Wisewomen & Boggy-boos

A Dictionary of Lesbian Fairy Lore

Jessica Amanda Salmonson
&
Jules Remedios Faye

BANNED BOOKS
Austin, Texas

A Banned Book

FIRST EDITION
First Printing

Copyright © 1992 by Jessica Amanda Salmonson and
                    Jules Remedios Faye

Published in the United States of America
By Edward-William Publishing Company
Number 292, P.O. Box 33280, Austin, Texas 78764

ISBN 0-934411-43-3

Thanks are extended to the following editors and publishers, in whose
magazines earlier versions of a few of the Wisewomen/Boggy-boo
tales, poems, and vignettes originally appeared:

Peggy Nadramia of *Grue Magazine*; Diane White and Jeanne Gomoll
of *Aurora Feminist Science Fiction*; Crispin Burnham of *Eldritch
Tales*; Richard H. Fawcett, publisher of *Fantasy & Terror*, edited by
Jessica Amanda Salmonson; Marleen S. Barr, guest editor of *International Women's Studies*; W. Paul Ganley of *Weirdbook*; and Thomas
Wiloch of *Grimoire*. Copyright © 1977, 1978, 1983, 1988, 1989, 1990.

Wisewomen
&
Boggy-boos

A

Abula: Also called Abulia, a fairy of derangement who robs women of their will-power, which she fashions into thistles, scattering their flaxen down to the wind. She is probably derived from the ancient Maenads, or divine madwomen. When she takes the form of Abassa, she is the Lizard Princess, whose garden is filled with gorgeous, twisted briars and jagged stones.

Abula's consort (in some tales, rival) is Aad, whose name is pronounced "Odd," the fairy of mesmerism. She appears at crossroads and invites women to her seraglio. A tale is told of a maid who in one moment was mesmerized by Aad, and in the next, her will was stolen by Abula. She wandered as a somnambulant, back and forth between the garden of Abula, and the palace of Aad, so that these fairies warred for her possession. The maid's name was Nihility, though the fairies called her Zerro.

One evening in the garden of Abula, Nihility pricked her finger on a rose, and awakened to her power. In a twinkling of a thought, the garden was devoured, and the nearby palace of Aad became mist. The fairies struggled to reclaim her, but she held them fast, one in each arm, and took them to a cavern where stood the loom of Fate. Under Zerro's guidance, Aad and Abula placed their locks upon the loom and began the restoration of the lost will of women. When their work is done, the world will be again secure for maenadic madness.

Acca the Fair: Called also Acca Halfdreamer. In Virgil's *Aeniad*, Acca is the comrade-lover of the Amazon Camilla.

After Camilla fell in battle, Acca was inconsolable. She withdrew into a distant forest where she sat weeping such tears that she was transformed into a fountain. Any woman who drinks of this fountain sleeps a hundred years.

Alice of the Coombe: A maiden of Cornwall who so despised the prospect of marriage that on her wedding day she turned herself into a mole and escaped underground. She is the first Cornish mole.

Allison Gross: The hag-form of Maisry (*q.v.*). She is beautiful to women, teaching them herb lore, midwifery, and witchcraft. But any man who sets eyes upon her believes she is ugly. She turns men into snakes and ties them around trees.

Anarchia: See Vulva.

Anna and the Miserable Man: Oh what a miserable man he was; oh what a dirty-old miserly man. He lived at the bottom of a foul lake and only came out of it at night, grumbling about the freshness of the air, cursing the beauty of the Moon and of midnight flowers, pained by the song of the nightingale. He swore a feeble oath to destroy all that was good in the world, for he was oppressed by kindness, and his tongue curled into a knot at the taste of honey, while music only grated on his waxy ears.

 The women of the land knew he lived on the bottom of the lake, for he left a track of filth after every night's sortie. Oh! What an unfortunate, misbegotten snail he seemed, leaving behind the gardens he had spoiled, and a trail of slime leading back to his putrescent waters.

 No one had ever seen the miserable man before Anna. Anna was very small at the time, young and innocent, and not yet the rowdy thing that girls become. She had gone out in the morning and discovered her flowers smashed into the ground. She had helped her mother plant them, had watched them grow from seeds, had cared for them every day. The sadness of their pointless destruction overwhelmed her child's heart and it seemed she would cry. But she caught sight of something beautiful: a track of slime capturing the morning light, turning it into a rainbow. "How very lovely," she thought, seeing it shimmering and shining beneath the sun! "How wondrously grand this feast for my eyes!"

Mother still slept when Anna began to follow the fallen rainbow. She had never seen one on the ground before, and was rather startled to discover that rainbows stank. But it was as beautiful as when raised in the sky and she wondered if it would lead her to a golden city in the Land of Fair like stories told.

It was a long way for Anna's short legs. She came to the lake by noon. Dead things floated near its banks and fungus grew big as trees. The lake was black and the wind sent terrible odors her direction. But to Anna it smelled like cabbage stew. She was the only child she had ever met who loved cabbage stew. Her mother grew big heads of cabbage and cooked them fresh with cream and barley. It was the best soup in the whole world even if it did smell something awful.

Anna thought it was too bad about the dead things floating in the water, but she was not afraid of death. She had been with her grandmother when the beautiful old wytche died, and had learned that it was not a terrible thing. It was a natural thing.

As for the fungus, it was not ugly to Anna. It was a marvel to behold, mushrooms big as trees, with blotchy pretty colors.

Something stirred beneath the surface of the black waters. Anna wondered if it were a magical fish. Her mother had told her a story about magical fish, and Anna had ever since longed to meet one. She walked to the edge of the dark waters and called, "Magical fish! Magical fish! I love you magical fish!"

The lake stirred vigorously, but if there was a magical fish, it did not answer.

"This is a beautiful place," remarked Anna, stroking the silky red fuzz growing on the trunk of a gigantic blue mushroom. Again the water stirred, this time more violently. When Anna asked of no one in particular, "Is this the edge of Fairyland?" the water roiled yet again, and she knew that whatever was in the lake could hear her. She sniffed the air and thought of her mother's boiling pot. She said, "It smells like stew. It makes me hungry."

The magical fish, if that were indeed what it was, made the water splash and pop and gurgle as though the stew were hot upon the fire. "That's a very good trick," Anna said with praise and awe. "Would you do it for me again?"

It was too much for the miserable man to contend. He burst up out of the water, beneath the light of day for the first time in untold years. He held his hands clapped to his ears and groaned and moaned and shouted, "Stop it! Stop it! How desperately I plead!"

When Anna saw the miserable man standing there in the water, she was immediately reminded of the scarecrow in the garden. She began to laugh at the sight of such a miserable man.

"Don't do that! Don't laugh!" he insisted in his hard, coarse voice. Anna fell silent, thinking it was bad of her to laugh at the way another person looked. "I'm very sorry," she said sweetly. "I think you look quite nice."

The miserable man screamed and splashed the black water with his fists. "I'm not! I'm not! I'm not at all nice! I'm mean and ugly and wicked and I eat little girls!"

"Ooo!" cried Anna, delighted. She clasped her hands. "That's a fine start to a story! Tell me the rest!"

The miserable man pulled at his hair and came sploshing toward the shore. He said, "I have sworn an oath to destroy all that is beautiful!" So saying, he picked Anna up and held her over his head. He threw her far out into the middle of the awful lake.

Anna made a huge splash. And where she landed the water became clear. She giggled and swam about, marvelling at how the blackness and stink drifted away from the strokes of her arms. In an ever-widening circle, the lake became purified by the ripples that grew away from Anna's body. The miserable man tried to leap out of the water, but he was too slow. The clean, clear liquid touched the hem of his robe. Cleanliness engulfed him. His dark raiment turned to white linen. His sooty, sallow face became pink and healthy. He covered his face with his hands but saw to his terror that they were uncalloused and smooth hands. He tried to scream, but it came out a melody.

Anna swam ashore and clambered on the bank. She told the miserable man she was sorry she spoiled his cabbage soup. But she promised to bring him some of her mother's. That did not cheer him. She left the miserable man alone, knowing she must return home before her mother worried much. Only once did she look back, and saw that even then the man looked miserable and sad and funny like the garden's scarecrow. She guessed he was miserable for a reason. But she never knew what the reason was.

Annie Boggles: A Boggy-boo (*q.v.*) that sniffs out women who are masturbating and licks their fingers clean. Annie is of indeterminant age, young-looking but with white hair. She has no hair in her armpits or on her cunt, but has hair on the soles of her feet. Annie's lovers are said also to grow fur under their feet, and to live to age one-hundred and twenty.

Atargatis: The first mermaid, or a water fairy, who disguises herself as an iridescent emerald- and lavender-scaled trout. She bites the hooks of fisherwomen and, though it causes her terrible pain, she allows them to pull her from the water, for all the fisherwomen gasp in awe of the beauty of the jeweled scales of Atargatis. Then, plumped full of their admiration, she leaps upward and plants a fat fish-lipped kiss upon their mouths before disappearing into the river bed. Forever after, those women have the gift of prophesy, be it for good or for evil.

Of all the women who have once drawn Atargatis from out the waves, she loves best the few that shed a silver tear for the apparently dying fish. Such a woman she transforms into a water-breathing creature and for three days, and three nights, they frolic fin to fin, chin to chin, belly to belly, stirring the river into a snowy froth. Then upon the dawn after the third night the transformation ends, the woman is washed ashore, but is thereafter web-toed and gifted with the ability to remain submerged between her lovers' thighs for immeasurable lengths of time.

B

Badb: Facetiously referred to as the opposite of Goodb, but her name is best pronounced "Bev." She is one of a trinity of fairy Amazons (along with Macha and Nemien, elsewhere given as Macha and the Morrigu) that haunt fields of battle. Badb takes the form of a raven and pecks the staring eyeballs of dead soldiers. See "The Dead Moon."

Barbie: A very bad fairy. Her barbs are invisible.

Barkity Kate: See Doggidy Kate.

Batty Picklock: A Boggy-boo who can enter any locked room that a girl sleeps in. Batty is a tall woman with green hair and seven breasts, but otherwise quite pretty. She lives in forests near pools, but can travel vast distances at night. Whoever's room she enters cannot awake until dawn, but writhes and moans with pleasure.

Bazzle Ratbone: Also given as Dazzling Ratty, most beautiful of the Rat-fairies. She carries messages to women in prisons. She has obsidian eyes and can see clearly in the blackest dark holes, thus serves as a guardian to women in lunatic asylums. She comes to women who are especially dispirited and, while they sleep, she climbs upon their pillows and sings in their ears, in the secret language of the Rat-fairies.

Bebhionn: Daughter of Teon of Celtic legend's Land of Maidens. She was a powerful maiden-giantess who warred against Aedh, to whom she had been unwillingly betrothed. He was a cruel, beautiful, effeminate giant who fought with spear. She routed his troops and expelled him from her nation, but died afterward of wounds. Her burial site was long known as the Mound of the Dead Maiden.

Billiwak: Or Spitting Billy, the inkpot sprite. She lives in ink fountains and causes dykes to write scathing editorials.

Bird-mender fairies: These grey-haired beauties reside at the periphery of every city and practice the ancient, sacred art of healing wild birds. Their houses and gardens are filled with birds of every kind. The Bird-mender fairies speak several bird languages fluently. Once a year, they revert to their natural form, setting all their mended birds free, and flying with them to visit the Queen of Birds.

Black Annis of Leicestershire: An incarnation of Dana (*q.v.*), a wisewoman or wycht (*q.v.*) vilified as a cannibal hag. Her cannibalism is an exaggeration of her fondness for menstrual blood. She comes to women on nights of the New Moon and drinks their menses.

Blackberry Fairy: In the summer she appears as a plump black fairy amidst the briars, enticing women to her embrace. She is the origin of the saying, "The darker the berry, the sweeter the juice."

> Merry Mary Blackberry fairy
> will you marry me
> Cows that play the live-long day
> have come to sample thee.

Bloddy Wot: Called also Bloody Wad, alternative names for Sanguina (*q.v.*).

Bluecap Cowy: Called also Knacky Blue. She can appear as a blue fairy-cow whose milk is sweet as honey, the drinking of which prolongs life. Only women see her. She travels to small villages as a lame lass in a blue cap (in some tellings, blue coveralls) and whoever gives her odd jobs and good food will live to be one-hundred twenty.

8

Boggy-boo: Same as Buggy-boo, Bugums, or Buggies. They are fairy women who love mortal girls, or who restore old women to girlhood, usually as an illusion. The Boggy-boos are either deformed, or attracted to deformity. Batty Picklock (*q.v.*) is a Boggy-boo with seven breasts. Annie Boggles (*q.v.*) has hair growing on the soles of her feet. Despite the oddities that mark the Boggy-boos, women who have seen them are struck mainly by their beauty.

Bonny Blackguard: A night-fairy, one of the paramours of Lolly Lilith (*q.v.*). She is sometimes to be seen only as a menacing shadow. She is in every brawl, throwing her fists and stirring women on. On All Hallow's Eve, she appears in dyke bars and buys everyone a round. Her money turns to leaves at dawn.

The Bone Maid: Also called Bonny Bones. She abhors food and is the patroness of diet-dykes.

Boxy: A train fairy. She lives in box cars and helps women wanderers. She boxes the ears of anyone giving trouble. Believed to be related to Box-car Bertha.

Brats: Good fairy-girls. They help human girls and animals. They are usually shaggy-haired. Though they look like children, they are six feet tall.

Broggity Jennet: A Scottish Boggy-boo (*q.v.*), called Blotch Janet in Cheshire, England. She can take the form of a speckled cat with prehensile tale and jumps from tree to tree. In her woman shape, she is red-haired and exceedingly freckled. With a wicked smile, she lures charwomen away from their chores, leading them all day and all night through wild forests; or, in towns and cities, from rooftop to rooftop, under the full moon. Come morning, worn and frazzled, they remember only her teasing smile. And the charwomen are thereafter restless and fierce and never return to domestic duties.

Brooms: The broom has been, since early ages, a symbol of women's servitude, not only in Europe, but throughout the world. In Japan the letter for "woman" is a stylized pictograph of a woman bent over with a broom. In Scandinavia, little brooms are dressed up in doll clothes to look like old women.

Wytches (*q.v.*) transformed this symbol into one of power, for which reason the wytche is often portrayed riding on a broom, sometimes with her female companion, the Black Cat. Freudians have tried to turn this feminist occult symbol into a penis substitute! Perhaps what Freudians perceived was the sexually charged nature of these women's orgies of magic and strength; but wytches used fingers and tongues, not their brooms.

Here's a pleasant rhyme sung by playful girls in medieval times, celebrating the wytche and her broom, taken from *The Oxford Nursery Rhyme Book*. It is a pleasant piece in showing that girls dreamed kindly dreams of joining the wytches.

> There was an old woman tossed up in a basket,
>   Seventeen times as high as the moon;
> Where she was going, I couldn't but ask it,
>   For in her hand she carried a broom.
> "Old woman, old woman, old woman" quoth I,
> "Where are you going to up so high?"
> "To brush the cobwebs off the sky!"
> "Can I go with you?" "Aye, by-and-by."

Brownies: A type of pixy that dresses all in brown, steals cookies from bakery shops, and sells them door to door. Some Brownies dress in blue and are called Bluebirds. They look like sweet little girls but are hundreds and hundreds of years old. If a Brownie falls in love with a mortal lass, she grows to maidenhood in only three or four days, returning to seduce her. But she can be a true Brownie never again, having given up immortality for love.

Buffalo Gal: A Moon-fairy of the American Wild West. She was celebrated in a famous song:

"Buffalo Gal won't you come out tonight,
Come out tonight, come out tonight.
Buffalo Gal won't you come out tonight
And dance by the light of the moon."

Native Americans called her White Buffalo Woman. She could leap from high mountains, and land lightly. She rode with braves on the buffalo hunt.

Bum Bee: Queen of the Bumble Bees. She rules a palace almost exclusively of women. Women fill all important offices and perform all important duties. Her Goddess is the Burnie Bee.

Burnie Bee: The Cornish Spirit of the Bee-hive. She defends bees, whose society honors that of the Maiden Land on the Isle of Fair. When women are threatened or attacked, the Burnie Bee sends her legions to sting the attacker to death.

The Caitskins: Meggy Caitskin, Tissy Caitskin and Alexis Caitskin were three warlike maids who wore the skins of cats and performed chivalrous deeds in service of women less warlike than themselves. They are believed to be forms of the goddesses called the Furies, whose names were Megara, Tisiphone, and Alecto. The origin of the Caitskins is given in the story of "The Wandering Gentle-women" (*q.v.*). In their old age, the Caitskins are said to have appeared to Hector Boethius, better known as Macbeth of Scotland.

Cat Anna: The deadly foe of Rat Anna (*q.v.*), though some say they were lovers. A nursery rhyme remembers her thus:

> "Patty Cat, Patty Cat,
> Sheath your claw;
> Rat-girl and Cat-girl
> Rollin' in the straw."

Cauldron: Magic pot of the wyches, itself anthropomor-phized as the Pot-mother of India, a very ancient God-dess. The cunt is the original Cauldron, in which tem-pests roil, and from which the world was born.

Changelings: What parents perceive their daughter to be once she has come out of the closet. In reality, the par-ents are changelings.

Christina Rossetti: A Poetry-fairy (see Rosy Crick), cele-brated in the poem "For the Biographer of Goblins."

Ever so pretty
Christina Rossetti
Wrote verses for me and you
  Of sweet little infants
  that died in an instant
Leaving their mothers blue.

Ever so snooty
Victorian beauty
Goes dancing with ladies grand
  Returning with lessons
  Regarding obsessions
With death — or a severed hand.

Churchmilk Gladdy: A Yorkshire Boggy-boo (*q.v.*) who guards nut groves. She looks old, but is exceedingly spry and handsome. She has six fingers on each hand, four toes on each foot, and passes her time smoking a pipe. When white-haired widows come to pick nuts, Churchmilk Gladdy sings:

"Be mine, by mine, my sweet old Goody
Sleep in the thicket with Churchmilk Gladdy."

Any widow who sleeps with her in the thicket wakes up young.

The Corn Fairy and the Gypsy: Kyzle Paff was a gypsy girl of Aberdeenshire. She travelled from place to place thieving and telling fortunes. She was a clever thief and her prophesies were always true. Yet once she fell on hard times, when nothing was worth stealing and all the futures she foretold were gloomy with foreboding.

Now Kyzle had a pony called Marzy Dotes that took her from place to place and was her best friend. Marzy was so beautiful that people said she was half fairy-horse or kelpie. And Marzy Dotes was a fierce pony, except with Kyzle Paff or children, so that no one else dared go near her.

But the sad fact is that no pony does well forever eating naught but nubbly grass, and Kyzle Paff feared her beloved Marzy was about to die. Therefore, in spite of her code only to thieve from the wealthy, she slipped one night into a poor farm-woman's cornfield, intending to take only enough corn to save her pony's life.

As she was about to pluck an ear, a tiny woman who looked to be of middle years, but only as tall as a one-year old child, appeared beside her, shimmering slightly, as fairies often do. She wore a yellow bonnet and a long straw-colored skirt, and climbed rapidly up the cornstalk to protect the ear.

The corn fairy seemed not actually to see Kyzle, but was fretful nonetheless, worrying about the corn.

So Kyzle moved to the next cornstalk thinking she would take that ear instead, but the little woman leapt to that one, and to the next one, and so on to the next, always guarding the corn-ear Kyzle wanted.

So Kyzle Paff perceived that even if her pony died, she dared not thieve from the fairy-guarded cornfield.

But when she woke in her sleeping-roll the next morning, she saw her pony eating fresh ears that had been neatly cut and shucked and arranged in a perfect circle.

After that, Kyzle's luck was good again. She told pleasant fortunes and was paid highly by people glad to hear them. She made enough money that she no longer had to steal. One day she found herself riding through a familiar place. Remembering the cornfield that fed her starving Marzy, she went to the house of the farmer-woman, thinking to pay for that corn.

The woman who came to the door was of middle years and pretty. She was tall and thin and wore a yellow dress; her hair was fine as cornsilk. She looked exactly like that corn-fairy, although not small. In her eyes showed a melancholy longing. Kyzle Paff said, "Mistress! A year ago, your cornfield fed my pony, and now I've come to pay you."

But the farm-woman refused to be paid, and told Kyzle, "That cornfield has lain fallow for seven years, for I am all alone and could not plant it."

"But it was filled with corn," said Kyzle.

"If you would stay and help me, gypsy, perhaps it will become so."

So Kyzle stayed and planted corn, for she knew that her own magic, and that of the farm-woman, had joined prophesy to the land, and bridged a span of time.

Couthie Wytche: "The Loving Witch," called also Bonny Wise. She comes as a nurse to a sick and dying woman, comforting her toward the end, and carrying her afterward to the Land of Fair.

Cramps: The penalty for annoying fairies. But some fairies ease cramps.

Crone: A very beautiful woman, divinely mad, often elderly. Also, a wytche (*q.v.*).

> A demented old woman writes poetry
> > She writes it on church walls and
> > > telephone poles
> > She carves it on tables in
> > > restaurants and halls
> > She prints it so tiny it
> > > falls into holes
> It glistens from caves wet and shiny.
>
> This demented old woman writes history
> > She writes it on moonbeams and
> > > sunlight and fire
> > She scrawls it when able in
> > > wishes and dreams
> > She makes it with needles or
> > > short lengths of wire
> Thrust into the shells of small beetles.
>
> The demented old woman writes morbidly
> > She tells of angry doom and
> > > white marble stones
> > Her ink is the sable of
> > > nightmare and gloom
> > Her pens are old hollowed out
> > > fingers and bones
> Wherever they point us we follow.

D

Danu: Originally the Great Goddess of Ireland, but dwindled to a warrior fairy. Her chief captains are Badb, Macha, and Nemien. Under these three were Dagda, Eire, and Fodla. And under them were Banba, Brigit and Eadon. This thrice three tripartate came together under full moons and new moons for lesbian orgies, either before or after battles, and into their midst came the Morrigu, Queen of Nightmares, ruler of the dark land beneath the Land of Fair. Lady Gregory says, "Among the other women were many shadow-forms and great queens; but Danu, that was called Mother of Gods, was beyond them all."

Dawn: A name for the Lion Maid, consort of Grandmother Bear, called Xanthursa, whom see.

The Dead Moon: In the Lincolnshire Fens they tell of the gloomy age when Men snared all the fairies and nothing beautiful remained in all the green world. There was war, and plague, and pillage. Selena, from her haven in the sky, heard the faint, far-away prayers of saddened fairies and mortal women. So she clad herself in darkness to walk up and down upon the earth. What she witnessed gave her sorrow.

When she passed through the foreboding Fens, a great serpenty root snagged her and drew her legs into the foul, wet bog. Men with armor made of iron, which fairies loathe, and armed with ashwood spears, stepped out from every tree and stabbed her and stabbed her, until she was all a speckled mass of blood.

The Fenmen had a great stone brought, borne by eighty slaves. They heaved it atop Selena's grave, and left a villainous sentry, the knight Sir William Wyke, who had a long black sword.

Now did the shattered world grow blacker, for there was not even a Moon to light the nights of terror. Tyrants ruled and tortured; one million perished of the plague; and the Fenmen pillaged all the more boldly. So evil were the men of this age that even Satan would not have them, and the oozy corpses warred and looted alongside their living brethren.

Upon the advice of a wisewoman, three maids took bronze weapons in their gentle hands, and clad their lovely bodies in armor made of bronze as bright as fire. And they set out for the Fens looking for the monolith that held the Moon fast in her grave.

They came upon Sir William Wyke, and begged him to do battle.

"I will fight thee, pretty maids," said William Wyke, and drew forth his long black sword.

As is well known, the Fair People cannot abide iron. But so wet was the Fen, Sir William's sword had gone to rust, and the world so dark he hadn't known. Therefore did the maids fight bronze against iron, and killed Sir William in his casque, and left him for the leeches and the worms.

Because Sir William had called them "pretty maids," and not "harridans" or "whores," his soul was freed from his decaying body, and wanders to this day in Lincolnshire, where it is known as Will o' the Wyke.

The three maids drew near the magic stone, infested though it was by the virulence of men. And in low incantations, they sang the charms that raised the stone. In spells sung lower still, they raised the slaughtered Moon. And without a sound at all, they stripped away Her dark cloak and kissed the many wounds of Her body, and healed them one by one.

Selena gazed anew upon the blighted world. The light of her restored the greeny pines. As she raised into the sky, the Fens were cleansed with silver glisten. But sorrow marked her brow, for to the three Fen Maidens she must say, "Now art thou soldiers, even as are men, and I cannot hold thee from what Destiny awaits. Thou art henceforth called Macha, and Morrigu, and Badb, and will haunt the battlefields as ravens. Good you'll do, and evil. Of all the Folk of the Fair Land, you will be most feared."

Come morning picked the Ravens midst the gnarly rooted stumps that once were mighty men.

Deegle: An evil pixy that lives in sidewalks and peers at you from cracks. If you step where she is hiding, she'll break your mother's back.

Demetria: The Pigeon-feeding fairy, appears to ignorant eyes as a weary hag. She cares for the children of Mother Mumbles (*q.v.*), who is her daughter. Grains of barley scatter from Demetria's gnarled hands and from the sleeves of her rumpled winter coat. At the Spring Equinox, her granddaughter pigeons gather in her coat. Demetria is carried to her palace in the Land of Maids, where she is a beautiful princess and the pigeons are dancing, laughing sprites.

Digger the Dungball: A male fairy who hangs out in lesbian bars and boasts afterward that it's the best way to get laid. He says, "Oh most beautiful goddess of handcuffs and knives, take me to your cabana." Once he approached Knocky-boo (*q.v.*) with this idea. She chained him to the bumper of her truck and drove him home.

Dim-dumpies: Two aged "sisters" or wisewomen (*q.v.*) who in their old age called themselves "dimpty dumps." Marion St. John Webb wrote of them thus:

The old ladies pass our gate
  Ev'ry mornin', dressed in brown.
One goes walkin'—*dimpty dump*—
  And wheels the other up an' down
In a Bath chair with a hood,
  Which they put up when there's rain.

Miss Dim-Dumpy singed a song,
  Till her sister made her stop,
'Case she tired herself too much,
  Reaching notes that's high on top.
An' the song she singed was called
  "Buy me a broom, my lady, buy!"
Mother says she singed so *old*
  It made her want to cry.

Dink Sander: A giantess. She guards crossroads and bridges. She quarries granite with her teeth. What she does with men is best left unwritten. It is Dink Sander who greets the spirits of gay women who have recently died. She asks them what road they seek—Heaven's or the Fair Land's—and always guides them true. With the sandpapery soles of her feet, she smooths their paths. With her sandpapery palms, she grinds their worries into dust. Those who choose Heaven enter by her snout. Those who choose the Fair Land enter by her mouth. Those who miss the mortal world are reborn through her belly.

Doggidy Kate: She is also called Barkity Kate, or Dogwina, related to Hecate. She is a fairy with a dog's head, or a dog's tongue, or a dog's tail, depending on what district she visits. It is said to be good luck to feed a stray bitch, because she may be Doggidy Kate's hound. If a woman is lost in the forest, Doggity Kate will save her. If it is cold, Doggidy Kate will sleep with her and keep her warm.

Doony-ma: Literally "the pony mother." She is a Boggy-boo who takes on the appearance of a pony, a beautiful maiden, or an elderly wytche. In the latter form she is said to live in a gingerbread house in the forest, or in a house with chicken's legs in the swamp. As a maiden she is the genius of thistles and nettles. Doony-ma protects girls who are fairy-touched. Once a little girl had climbed high into an enormous oak and was unable to get down. The Doony-ma appeared as a granny and held out her apron, saying, "Leap into this, my sweet!" The little girl leapt into the old woman's apron and was swallowed in its folds. The girl then awakened safely in her bed.

The Doony-ma is a Scottish relative of Irish Dana (*q.v.*). In some regions there is still current a belief that she is a rheumy-eyed hag weeping constantly for the condition of women in the modern world. She can be conjured by a ritual incantation:

> In her eye there is a tear
> In the tear there is a dolphin
> In the dolphin is a worm
> In the worm there is a pebble
> In the pebble is a hollow
> In the hollow is a pearl
> In the pearl there is a seed
> That grows into the Doony-ma
> And when she sees the world
> She weeps a tear
> In which there is a dolphin,
> a worm,
> a pebble,
> a hollow,
> a pearl,
> and a seed.

Doppelgänger: One's double. Especially one that comes as a lover. One Hallowe'en seventy years ago, Lizette Woodworth Reese wrote:

> "Two things I did on Hallow's Night:
> Made my house April-clean;
> Left open wide my door
> To the ghosts of the year.
>
> Then one came in. Across the room
> It stood up long and fair—
> The ghost that was myself—
> And gave me stare for stare."

Dreams: Where truth is made.

Dust-mite fairies: They make their nests in dusty corners under the beds of lesbians. When the mattress begins to creak and bounce and noisy moans and screams issue from above, the Dust-mite fairies are awakened and begin ecstatically to roll about in little circles beneath the bed. Soon they are joined by other dust-mite fairies who leap and prance and revel until the noises and activities above quieten down. Then all the little Dust-mite fairies fall back to sleep and drift away in dreamy rest.

E

Eency: A giantess. Inverted forests grow between her legs and in her armpits. Her paramour is Weency. In olden times they were called Earth Mother and Earth Grandmother.

Elle-maids: Scandinavian fairies who live in groups of three, seven, or thirteen, especially in ancient mounds. They are exceedingly beautiful and have long golden hair that wraps all about their bodies. They are said to be unable to walk backwards or tell lies. They sing beautifully. Usually they are invisible to mortals but on special festive occasions they may be seen dancing upon their mounds and around old megaliths. A woman who joins them will be given a magic drink from a cow's horn and pass the night in glorious ecstacy. But a man who tries to join them will be met by the smallest Elle-maid who strikes him dead with one blow, no matter how strong he is.

Emilida: The Massachusetts fairy of elegant spinsterhood, reported from Amherst and nearby environs. She surrounds herself with a pleasant clutter of lace and foolscap paper and clockwork ballerinas. She invests women's pens and quills with magic, and is the spirit of poetry and solitude.

Empusae: Sea-women that can take the form of birds of prey or of wild seahorses, sometimes personified in art as unicorns leaping violently in ocean breakers. They are associated with death ships: vessels carrying prisoners, slaves, plague, or otherwise with doleful destinies. A tale is told in Australia of a prison ship that sank among the reefs. The women alone survived, each believing they had ridden horses to the nation of beautiful Queen Lamia, and lived there many years. When they were warned that to stay longer meant they must be transformed into Sirens (*q.v.*), all but two elected to return to the mortal world. The horses brought them upward to a stormy shore, where they found that only moments had elapsed and the prison ship was still breaking against the reef. The corpses of the two women who chose to stay behind were washed ashore in close embrace.

Evie Pippin: One of the Fruit Fairies, genius of the apple trees, and consort of Hunky Buttons (*q.v.*). She has long, brown, gnarly limbs and a ruddy complexion. In the winter she scarcely moves, but in spring she is agile and swift and seduces Hunky Buttons with wicked pleasures. Together in the autumn they build castles of apple and cherry leaves, enticing country dykes with sweet fruit wine and kisses. Who sleeps with them in the leafy mould has thereafter a cunt that smells of apples, and cherry scented menses.

The Evil Jinn: My friend and I walked for months across rugged, ruined terrain. We had stretched the contents of our lunch bag to last that whole time, for there were only impure resources along the way. At last we were down to our last two pieces of cheese.

A man came up behind me. He must have known I had the cheese in my pocket. He said, "Please, could you spare some food!" He had a nice West Indies accent, but otherwise was as disgusting as any other beggar. He was black as coal and not much cleaner.

"We have barely enough for ourselves," I said. "Please leave us be."

"Did not the poor Samaritan feed Jesus?" he asked. I noticed something odd about his mouth. His white teeth were widely spaced. His tongue was bright red. "And didn't she live forever in the kingdom of paradise?"

I gave him the cheese, though I knew my friend and I would starve. "Take it," I said. "Only, leave us alone."

He took the two slices of cheese, looked them over, then threw them on the ground. "I really wanted something else," he confessed.

Exasperated, I hurried to rejoin my friend, who was not speaking. We walked up a hill to a cemetery and started across it toward an airfield in the distance. We had seen an airplane in the sky before our quest began. That was the reason we had set out in the beginning. Our quest was nearing its end — though, if the airport was as lifeless as the rest of the world we had passed through, we would have to make the long trek back home without so much as a slice of provision.

The blackfellow followed us. We ignored him. After a while, we ceased to be afraid and forgot him utterly. My friend was still not speaking to me, although I could perceive no reason for her to be angry. I began to pout and dawdle and thereby fell behind. It was then that the blackfellow came up to me again.

"What I really wanted," he explained, "was for your friend to bear my children. Her skin is almost as dark as mine and therefore our blood should be compatible."

"Why take this up with me?" I asked. "I do not speak for my friend who, until this moment, you have not seemed to notice."

"It is true I was attracted to your golden hair," he said. "I would trade my freedom for a white woman! A brother told me so. But I would not dilute my race more than the plantation rapists have already done. I am more of a patriot than that! Therefore I chose your partner."

"My friend is Italian," I pointed out. "Unlike myself, she has deigned not to walk beneath our umbrella. Thereby the sun has turned her black. Still, she does not look of your race, so I doubt the sincerity of your statements."

"You are right," he said. "I am not sincere in my prejudices. I am not even truly black. I am actually an evil jinn. I chose to appear to you as a blackfellow be-

24

cause I knew that in your profound liberalism, you would not be able to turn me away. Whereas, were I white, you would have had nothing to do with someone as obnoxious as me."

"Why," I asked, disbelieving his story, "would an evil jinn discuss with me his fondness for my friend?"

"When an evil jinn mates," he explained, "no copulation is involved. The method is quite simple: He finds two women together and distracts one by monopolizing the other. Were I to talk to your friend, she would see through my ruses as you have seen through them. In that case, it would be you and not she that I impregnated."

To my friend's left there grew a small tree. On one of its branches two babies appeared, sitting side by side. They had appeared from nowhere, one after the other, with little "popping" sounds like that of a linen cloth pulled taut. They were a dazzling orange. My friend was instantly maternal toward them, and cooed love at them in their tree. They visibly grew on her attention.

"Ah," said the evil jinn with a note of pride. "My children!"

I ran to my friend's side, who had shrunk as much as the babies had grown. They were now fat cherubs and had turned a pallorous blue. "My friend!" I addressed. "Can you not see this is no natural birth? You were not pregnant five minutes ago. Now you are the mother of twins! Pray, let us destroy the infant evil and be on our way!"

But my friend was convinced of the normality of her good fortune. Indeed, she informed me in specialized medical terminology that she remembered every month of her healthy gestation with crystal clarity—although she confessed there was no memory of having slept with a man in her entire life.

"You shall not convince her," the evil jinn whispered in my ear. "I placed into her mind all she need ever know of pregnancy, and then some. She is, in fact, a walking medical encyclopedia. I never read it myself, you understand, lazy jinn that I am, but I transferred its content direct to her subconscious, and directed her consciousness to select whatever knowledge would convince her of a natural pregnancy and childbirth."

I saw that my friend was truly smitten. The baby jinns absorbed her tenderness and good will until she was frightfully gaunt. Whereas they had grown large and were as healthily pink as dogs' tongues.

"Please see the truth!" I pleaded. "The supernatural offspring are killing you! Think of our love! Overcome this hypnotism!"

"A virgin birth," she said dreamily. "Partheno . . . partheno . . ." I could almost see her subconsciousness thumbing through its medical encyclopedia.

"Think of our love!" I reiterated desperately.

My friend reached into her backpack and calmly withdrew the knife we had brought for protection. She held it above her head and proclaimed, "I was not fooled for an instant!" She stabbed the first baby in its belly and it popped out of existence. My friend was at once more healthy. The evil jinn, however, doubled over as though the knife had struck *his* belly. My friend then stuck the other baby through the brain. It, too, vanished with a brief sound of an implosion. The evil jinn fell to the ground, rolling about and clutching at his head, and finally died.

Later, at the airport, we purchased tickets to fly home. We could never have survived the walk back, having been deprived of provisions. It was a quick flight. It had been a disappointing quest.

F

Fabulina: The Immortal Child of Fair, a naïve voyeur-fairy who observes cruelty, horror, and lust, but remains unmoved. She neither hates, nor judges, nor desires. Her playmate is Ursalina, the Little Bear. In her ancient mortal form she was Atalanta, the child abandoned on a hillside and suckled by a bear. Fabulina is also the Genius of Autistic Children, who in the middle ages were mistaken for changelings, and typically abandoned.

Faggots: Bundles of twigs, used as kindling. In the middle ages, due to the burning of wytches, faggot came to mean "wife," as in, "How's your old faggot, John." "Oh, she's fine." In recent times, gay men, attempting to usurp women's history — as Dionysus strove to usurp the mysteries of Demeter — have claimed that they were the faggots used to set wytches aflame. But as a derogatory term from heterosexual men, faggot was, like "Nelly" and "Sissy," a method of calling gay men the worst thing men could think of: "woman."

Familiars: Harmless pets, sometimes with magic powers, kept by wychts (*q.v.*). See "Pets Given in Evidence of Old English Witchcraft."

Fantasia: An Egyptian poetess, who drew a marvelous account of the fall of Troy, which Homer later copied. Her spirit lives on in the Land of Fair, where she is guardian of the Sacred Texts. She travels from dream to dream, in the minds of sleeping maidens, planting the seeds of her fabulous stories. Dreamers when awakened commonly forget Fantasia's inspirations. Others are driven to obsession, and seek Fantasia in the waking dreams of opium and art.

Fett Frunners: In Roumanian fairy lore, Fett Frunners was the granddaughter of a priest. A tyrant forces every household to provide a son for the army, but the priest had no son. In a version prepared by Mrs. Andrew Lang, Fett Frunners disguises herself as a boy and sets out to join the king's army. He suspects she is not the man she seems, and with his mother's aid, sets a series of snares intended to force Fett Frunners to reveal her true sex. She evades each test, and becomes captain of the armies. She then sets off to fight an ogre and save a damsel in distress. She not only saves the damsel, but falls in love with her, purports to change her sex, and marries her! Several variants of this story have been "retold" in fairy tale collections, but only Mrs. Lang's preserves the lesbian content.

Figalia: The aggressive, pansexual Fig-fairy, who is fond of women, men, and horses. She has a purple face and multiple tongues of blue. Her cunt is sweet as candy. She usually manifests herself as plump and pretty, but is also known in a hag aspect, shriveled and brown. She is sometimes symbolized as a fig-leaf in paintings and on statuary, coddling her favorite spaces.

Fire-breathing women: See "Kro and Kraken."

Firefly Fairy: A minute avenger who burns out the eyes of rapists. In her gentle aspect, she causes women to glow with passion for one another.

Fishwife: See Atargatis.

Fook: A past-time of lesbian fairies, also called yump and yolly, played most commonly in pairs.

Fritzi Flüttermaus: A wingéd Rat-fairy (*q.v.*) who can appear as a grey-haired wisewoman. She gains access to the highest towers where women are imprisoned. She gnaws the bolts and locks and serves as a messenger. In medieval times she was the patron fairy-saint of women thieves and of children living in sewers. In World War II, she helped Jewish women escape from camps. She even sent her children into the camps and allowed them to be eaten.

Fudge Fairy: A very plump fairy. She lives in kitchens and helps clean pots.

G

Gloriana: Virgin Empress of the Land of Fair (*q.v.*). Edmund Spencer wrote in 1560, in Book Eight, Canto Three, of *The Faerie Queene:*

> "Faire May-lady with garlands all bespread
> Danced spritely into Gloriana's bed
> And of their lovely friendship fully glade
> Shewd seemly grace, their faces ruddy shade."

Gobble Oggy: The pool-table fairy of lesbian bars. Only drunken lesbians can see her. She hides in the pool table and pushes away all the balls from the pockets, excepting only the cue ball and the eight-ball, which she snatches and pulls in. After the closing hour, she and other tomrigs (*q.v.*) dance and rut upon the pool table green.

Goldy Yarrow: She comes to maidens pissing in meadows and says, "Give me your piss!" If the maiden stays squatting and lets all her piss soak into the grass, Goldy Yarrow runs a long distance, shouting:

> "The idea that a thick-bottomed maid
> Denied poore Gold by gladness be sprayed!"

But if the maiden stands up tall and allows her piss to spray between her legs, Goldie will run forth for a shower. Any woman who so pleases Goldie Yarrow is given wytche-knowlege and lives to one-hundred twenty.

Grandmother God: Long before earth or stars were born, old grandmother god felt a churning in her belly and she was stirred to dance. Her great long claws uncurled slowly from the pit of her fists and raising in perfect arcs her fingertips traced spirals through the heavens. Round and round she stretched and reached circling up and out then sinking down and down. Her thighs rolled thunderously, pulling to the rhythmic waves that poured from naked thigh to pumping foot. Her feet spread wide and wider still with the pounding, pulsing dance. Muscles rippled across shoulders, unfurling against outer edge of darkest wing. Legs, hair, wings curved out to encompass all of creation in a rich steaming embrace. And from her throat came the spelling of her name which she sang across the skies in undulating tones flowing and overflowing away along streamers of resonating sound. All around her, droplets of pearly sweat began to fly from beneath her generous breasts as she shook and swayed and rocked heaven in her salty lap. And from those drops she spun a living net of stars and planets and world upon world came boiling to life.

Grandmother Junk: This is the tale Wendy told Jane when they were children. As I wasn't there, I've changed it a bit. There once was a grandmother who lost her head. She looked for it in the bowling alley and found a huge black ball to sit upon her shoulders. Near the baseball field, she misplaced her left leg and hopped around until she located a splendid bat which served. Her stomach was forgotten somewhere so she replaced it with a toaster. When she lost her kneecap, she put a doorknob in its place. When her belly button vanished, she got a buzzer. Discovering that she had misplaced the toes of her right foot, she looked for them under the hood of a car and found sparkplugs instead. When her arms were gone one morning, she mistook a wooden spoon and wooden fork for them, and fitted these on snugly. Noticing other old people had humps upon their backs, she attached a breadbox to herself and it stuck nicely. Her breasts had sunken over the years, so she built them up with a teapot on the right and a coffeepot on the left. One day, when she had a friend over, the grandmother removed two slices of bread from her hunchback and toasted them in her belly. She made tea and coffee in her teats. She tossed a salad with her strange arms. After lunch, she and her friend played cricket on the lawn, using the bowling ball and baseball bat. When she died, nobody buried her. They donated her to a thrift shop. By this means, she was able to do good works even after death.

Granny Bundle: Either a wytche or an elderly Boggy-boo with long fingers, tall spine, and rheumy eyes. She goes from door to door with her scarf tied into a bag carrying scrap lace, chipped ivory buttons, golden thread, brittle turtle-shell combs, green shoelaces, violet crystal eye-cups, silver salt-spoons, and curious little idols of forgotten goddesses. She unfolds her bundle inside the door of any house were mothers bid her enter. A young mother who sees these tragic odds and ends is stricken with sadness and nostalgia for a world she is convinced she's never seen. But a little daughter leaps with joy, awe, and remembrance of the Land of Fair. Any item she selects she cherishes until old age, and clings to in sad moments, and is healed.

Granny Obia: A famous wytch.

> Sometimes I awake and see my Granny Obia
> Brewing wolfsbane hemlock tea
> Shaping spells to defend me
> Making bullies jump and flee—
> O, my Granny Obia.
>
> One hundred and thirty-three was Granny Obia
> Laid to rest beneath a tree
> Root of hemlock through her knee
> See that spirit floating free?
> That's my Granny Obia.
>
> Granny's eyes at windows peering;
> Granny's fingers grip the eaves;
> Granny's ears to chimney hearing;
> Granny's breath of crumbled leaves;

Granny's nose to kettle smelling;
Granny's nails as black as coal;
Granny's lips to my ears, telling
Granny's secrets to my soul:

"Greet the wicked beast of marvels
Sup the bitter feast of shades
Kiss the sable queen of darkness
Weave the magic in your braids.
Two in one we both shall be," says Granny Obia
"I am you and you are we."

Granny combing my hair sweetly
Twine the braids in circles neatly
Murmurs gorgeous spells discreetly
Till I rise and shout with glee
"I am Granny Obia!"

Gullveig: As reported by Dumézil, her name means "Madness of Gold," because her flesh was made of gold. Gullveig may be a Scandinavian symbol of insanity, conquering like Dionysus by altering morality in subtle or sinister patterns. What is clear is that women liked her, men did not. She inspired women to theft, adultery, and lesbianism. She was challenged by viking men who pierced her with spears all the way through her belly, but she would not die. She was thus consigned three times to death by fire, and three times survived.

Gwracher Ribbon: A Welsh lesbian banshee mentioned both by Katherine Briggs and John Rhys, and having some connection to the Mother-goddess Ana or Danu (*q.v.*). Gwracher Ribbon strides invisibly alongside the woman she wants to warn of impending death. When they come to a cross-roads or a river, she beats the ground or splashes the water, shrieking unhappily, "My wife! My wife! My wife!"

H

Haggardly Beth and the Black Hour: "The Black Hour," said my aged informant, "was an event that you or I should know for a common eclipse 'twa happening today. To folk of 1432, Year of our Lord, 'twa an hour when all hope was lost and sure doom was expected for they of plague-ravaged Scotland."

"You promised a tale of the supernatural," I said, placing my tape recorder beside her, "not of common superstition."

"Ah, leddie," said the old woman, "I doubts they are separate things. Today we can understand an eclipse or the ravages of a disease. But much else there is unkenned. 'Tis a supernatural yarn I have to spare ye, of that be sure; one which took place during that hour of horror and darkness when all Scotland waited for God's fist to flatten out the links and sweep away the whole of the dear land. 'Tis a tale without explanation, I can tell ye that; but who is to say it wouldna be explained in a wiselike future time? For ye, 'twill be mere legend, an auld story jumbled-up and added-to by distance of time. But on times I's a thinkin' a folk-memory can be clearer as regards auld times, more so than this mornin' paper catches the import of yestereen's events. What I shall tell ye is God's truth, no less; as true in its unkenned portions as about the eclipse. That much can be verified with astronomers if ye wouldna trust a tale of common people."

"I'm eager to hear the story," I said, enthused by its introduction.

"Well then, not all the Scotch waited passively and despaired as the sky went black in broad of day. Many set out to save the world by finding and burning witches, merrily as could be. I fancy I mighta burned that day, had I lived then; oftimes I dream I perished indeed, but am reborn to tell the tale. Any thrawart gal with a gobber tooth, a crooked back, and a dog lucklessly named Dick or Peck or Sam—names for Auld Cootly his evil self— were fair game to horrified Christians. So much the worse if the puir auld soul couldna make much sense when speakin' and is apt to agree to all sorts of improbable ideas, or thinks up some unlikely deed with her crippled mind, and wonders sure if she didna do it.

"More terrible still if she practiced simple medicine of the auld kind. She might've had neebors knockin' up from time to time, men and women needful of an herb or poultice; and in good times this is fine. Whether the remedy worked or nay; whether the folk be friendly or fearful of her knowledge—in times of trouble, 'tis easy to change one's thinkin' for the worse as regards a crone like that. And what if she disliked the kirk and the kirkyard save at night, with no one about to give her a hard look? Mightna she be gathering gravesoil for her bitter herbs? She might. Or people might only think she might. And what else? What if she did worship some auld god from before the time of Christians? Who does not, in the guise of Saint or Fairy?

"Well, and well, Haggardly Beth fitted all these de- grees. She kept a dog named Peck, as toothless as she. He was always fetching things home to her, useless things he found lying about. And didna't make him seem a witch's familiar running errands? Didna he attract the hands of children who liked to stroke his back? That's a thing of glamour, sure and sure's can be. Auld Beth had a mole on her thigh as big as a twopenny. Wouldna thing like that suckle an auld dog?

"She gathered herbs and grew others and mixed 'em in secret recipes that'd stop or start anybody's shattin' just as she decreed. And more than once a young leddie come about for a special tea that done away with an unexpected pregnancy by a laird she couldna hope to marry.

"And didna she talk to fairies? She believed she did. Who knows? And when she was spittin' angry, she could cuss a storm, and always made a terrible oath on the head of the horse-goddess. If she wa denied a crust of bread off a rich baker, she could screech such a horrid promise of his being trampled in his bed by ten black stallions! He might throw water on her from his piss-pot to get her to go away, and think no more about curses. But if such a man as this wa to die of the plague, as a fourth of the country died that year, someone had to wonder if 'twan't the horses after all.

"Then came the day that fell darker than a black night. And those who looked to see the sun gobbled up by some monster, aye, they went blind and never saw light again. 'Twa an awful wailing, people fallin' in the street and beseeching the Trinity. And men with swords and thick staves set forth well before the sun was full blotted out, intending to reverse the process by doing harm to all imagined witches in the burgh.

"The Black Hour became well-lit with fires. In every blaze writhed and shrieked some auld hag. And lo! the sun began by stages to recover itself. So the witchhunters felt they did well.

"Haggardly Beth was dragged toward such a pyre, her dog Peck gumming at the heels of the persecutors, yowfing and yarving to small effect, except to get his neck broke by a big man's booted heel. Beth yawped worse than the dog, for love of the tike that was kickin' in the throes of a painful death. Beth feared the fire, but lamented her dog the most. She set to cursin' better than ever before, callin' them a pack of bullyraggin' libbet-limmers. And she yawped with a vehemency that made the men lay off a bit, for they was afrighted to touch such a spindly hag animated by so much hate.

"Ye want what wee speck of life I have left, do ye?' said she. 'Ye want me as dead as puir Peck what never hurt a rabbit nae bit a child but loved everyone and me most? Ye evil limmers! And ye fear the Black Hour? And ye fear the Black Death? Ay, have I lived one-hundred years; and ay, I recollect the same plague a century anon; and nay, killin' me shan't stop it. But I swear ye shall never fall from the loathly plague, for ye shall die in the bloom of malicious manliness. Ye shall fall before the sun comes out from that hole! I curse ye and curse ye well! If there be justice from God and Epona and the Fair Folk, too, I call them all to trample ye 'neath hoofs of steel! Ye wish me burnt in yonder pyre? No need to haul me to it! I go myself on my own bent legs!'

"And so she hobbled to the flames and climbed right in, screaming, 'The mares! The mares! Oh, the beautiful mares of the Black Hour!'

"And sure to be told, there wa horses raging blindly through the street of the burgh! There wa nine of them. They wa black and sleek and their eyes wa wild. The persecutors wa frozen to their spots, shakin' in their trews. They wa knocked about like nine-pins, then the pounding hoofs went on and the horses disappeared.

"Haggardly Beth stood in the blazes cackling without pain and without surprise. Then she collapsed, sacrifice to her own magic. Even so, she raised herself up, charred black and oozy-like. She rose to arms and knees, flames all about her. She gazed out from the blazes at a trampled man who was crawling toward her though all his limbs wa broken and his cheek shorn off. They looked into each other's eyes, and Haggardly Beth told him, 'Is it justice after all? Indeed it is. Therefore shall I let the sun return upon the links for now.'

"The trampled man lived long enough to tell the story. It was repeated across the countryside. It was widely believed that the Black Hour would never have ended but for a witch forgiving her persecutors. Such is the tale of

Haggardly Beth and the Black Hour; such is the truth to be told."

I said, "It's a fine story to be sure, but too easily explained. The witch was credited for causing, then delivering from, a darkness you and I know was of natural source. Is that a supernatural tale? As for the horses, mightn't they have broken from some barn and raced through the street in fright and confusion?"

"A natural horse wouldna run by night," said the old woman. "But believe as ye require. Ye asked for a tale to put in that tape machine, and now ye have it. If it won't do, it won't do. Only, 'ware of insultin' an auld witch." She laughed with teasing, false menace. "It grows dark as we talk. And ye must trudge the length of the village alone. Listen as you go! Listen for the clop of hoof!"

Harly Marl: A saintly Boggy-boo, one of the shortest in stature, but broadly built. She attends the bedsides of lesbians injured in motorcycle accidents. She dances for them and shows her pubes. She may be many fairies, spirit-manifestations of women's leather jackets, or she may be a single fairy able to be many places at once.

Hazden Mot, the Nugly Little Woman: She controls mist and fog and can call pestilence from the swamp. She lives among the roots of hazel trees and is either the lover or sister of Churchmilk Gladdy (*q.v.*), or else Gladdy herself in a darker manifestation. In the Middle Ages Hazden Mot was "the nugly hag-wife," who, fearless during the plagues, nursed dying women. But she was falsely accused of causing the deaths and therefore withdrew to "a secret land beneath the bogs." In another story, she was herself spotted with plague, and was therefore called Piebald Hazle, and with a magic flute called all the infected rats into the swamp, where she drowned them, and herself. Belief in Hazden Mot has lately been revived in Edinbourough and nearby villages, where she is reported to have nursed gay men, and led their spirits to the Secret Land.

Hummingbird fairies: Small species of New World fairy that pollinates lily-scented cunts, causing lesbians to give birth to swarms of honey bees, lady beetles, dragonflies, and hummingbird fairies.

Hunky Buttons: A tall, butch, beautiful fairy with teats as big as watermelons, fists as big as grapefruits, and a clit as big as a fig. However, Hunky Buttons is terribly shy. She is seen wandering back roads of country places. She is the consort of the genius of apple trees, Evie Pippin (*q.v.*). She is herself the genius of cherries.

Hyena: In medieval folklore, the hyena was believed a creature of damnation. They were laughing females whose aberrant orgies were an abomination unto God. The ancient Greeks called lesbian sorceresses *hyenae*, and believed that in former lives they had been men. In Leonora Carrington's short story "The Debutante," the hyena is a friend to girls, who frees them from authoritative restraint. See "Leonora's Hearing Trumpet."

I

Ik: The Wimp-fairy. When asked to help move boxes, she whines, "Ew, it's too heavy." She hates to get dirty or break a fingernail. She is cute as a bug's ear but has a grating voice, and sniffs too much. Once upon a time, Ik was driving about in her sporty fairy cart, wearing her flourescent pink summer shift. The Burnie Bee (*q.v.*) innocently hitched a ride, but when Ik saw her, she cried out, "Ew! A bee!" and tried to swat her with a beauty college pamphlet, thereby driving into a ditch.

Burnie Bee was so deeply offended, she simply flew away and left Ik stuck in the ditch. Ik sat in the hot cart for an hour, whining, "Ew, I'm sweaty." She finally got out of the cart and began to walk home in her high heel shoes. "Ew, I broke my heel." She limped for half an hour longer, then said, "Ew, my stockings," and sat down on a rock to cry.

In a nearby field of fairy clover was Lou Lambkins (*q.v.*). She heard the forlorn wails and frolicked to Ik's side. Although Lou was smaller than a kitten, she carried Ik safely home. Ever since that day, when Ik cries, "Ew!" the little ewe comes running.

Inferna: The living heart of Grandmother God (*q.v.*), an endless country of terrible beauty, wherein gather the shades of forgotten goddesses and murdered fairies. In former times Inferna was the abode of the souls of Maenads and nymphs.

Iris: A Flower-fairy. She transformed herself into a flower of marshes and shallow pools in order to remain near Water Lily, her true love. Old myths say they became flowers to escape the lusts of men, but probably they gave men no thought. The aquatic Iris can be any color of the rainbow, but is generally yellow. Her twin sister, who is also named Iris, but nearly always of a lavender hue, lives upon dry land, in company with Lily White, a Death-fairy.

Either of the Irises is apt to exude a hallucinatory fragrance on nights of the rare blue moon. When lesbians catch the scent, they dream of ecstatic and sensual adventures, that might be true.

Isle of Maids: Called also the Maiden Land (*q.v.*), an island or perhaps a peninsula in the Land of Fair (*q.v.*), or an archipelago consisting of the mountain peaks of the country under the sea ruled by Queen Lamia (*q.v.*). A belief in such an island has persisted since earliest antiquity, and has been identified at different times as Lemnos, Samothrace, Lesbos, Feminie and Canabee of Spanish Romance, Hesperia or Tritonia (today called the Canary Islands), Queen Charlottes (where Captain Cook found a matriarchal colony), Atlantis, Mantinino (which Columbus sought in the Carribean), Ireland, the Isle of Skye, Java, El-wak-wak of the Arabian Nights, and many others.

Ixy Pigsy: A pixy girl with a little round snout. She steals human girls' underpants. When one sock is missing, Ixy Pigsy has it.

J

Jackie Lantern: An alternative name for (or consort of) Joan the Wadd (*q.v.*). She is a Will o' the Wisp, called also The Maid of Ireland. A nursery rhyme, the meaning of which is no longer widely admitted, is still sung:

> "Jackie Lantern, Joan the Wadd
> Who tickles the maids and makes them mad
> Light me home, the weather's bad."

Jackie is today made from pumpkins on All Hallow's Eve, the Wytche's New Year, to light porches, that all good wytches find their way.

Jammy Buggums: The Pajama Party Fairy. She sits invisibly among any group of giggly girls and encourages them first to talk about really sexy stuff, then to talk about really scary stuff, then to shiver under their covers two by two in one anothers' arms.

Jane and Emily Jane, the Bedknob Fairies: A pair of fairies who look just like bedknobs, round and hard and brown, about the right size to climb upon and squeeze into the cunt.

Jane the Ladder: She is the origin of the saying "don't walk under a ladder." She challenges lesbians to climb the rungs of her enormous legs. Although a handful of dykes have gotten lost in the folds of her cunt, not one has gotten farther.

Jenny Gobbergreen: An old wytch (*q.v.*) with but one tooth, and that tooth green. Any woman who feels unloved, and who says to herself, "I have never been loved; I will never be loved," is apt to be visited by Jenny. "I love ye," says Jenny. "I will love ye now and forever, if ye will have old Jen." Who rejects her is indeed lost of love for all her terrible life. But whoever welcomes Jenny Gobbergreen will never again feel disheartened. For Jenny will remove her one tooth, then vanish into it, becoming the beautiful Green Maid. Therefore any widow or spinster with a beautiful garden is said to be lovers with the Maid of Green.

Joan the Wadd: A pisky (pesky, or pixy) of Wales and Cornwall. Sometimes she is nothing but a Will o' the Wisp, but as a pisky she likes to get under the covers and tickle women's feet.

⇥ K ⇤

The Kaifeng Begger Women: "I'm open for business!" said the storyteller. We heard her tell this story in the streets of Nanking.

This story was first told by an itinerant nun of the Sung Dynasty (said the storyteller), so it may be true. Once were two beggar-women who begged in the streets of Kaifeng. People put coins in their dented bowl. By this means the beggar-women had barely enough to eat. One day the beggar-major spotted them and said, "You have to pay such-and-such to beg in this place."

"But we make barely that much for ourselves."

"Then beg over there, for that only costs such-and-such."

"We have tried begging there, and get nothing."

"This is my down-payment," said the beggar-major, emptying their bowl in his hand. "I'll check on you tomorrow."

That evening the beggar-women had nothing to eat. They clung to one another underneath a bridge, shivering and hungry. The moon poked through a crack in the bridge, illuminating the dented bowl. The moonlight revealed a tiny old woman in the bowl. The beggar-women had fallen asleep, and did not see her. She ran around inside the bowl, then hopped up and down, then made circle-motions with her arms. She took a glimmering powder from her little apron pocket and tossed it all about.

The next day the women were out begging. The beggar-major came that afternoon and put his fingers in their dented bowl. He grabbed the coins, but could not pull them out. The bowl came away and was stuck to his fist. In fact, his arm was slowly disappearing deep into the bowl. The beggar-major howled and hopped. He was in such an hysterical state, no one could understand what he was yelling. Passersby thought it looked like a one-armed beggar's song and dance. They threw coins in the laps of the beggar-women sitting near.

The beggar-major could still feel his arm and hand, although the bowl seemed to have devoured him to the shoulder. He felt the coins still clutched in his fist. Finally he had the good sense to let go of the coins. The bowl fell the length of his arm, and he was safe and whole.

That evening the beggar women ate hot noodles. They slept under the bridge, their arms around each other, dreaming pretty dreams. Inside the bowl was the tiny woman, watching over them.

The next day, the beggar-major came with two thugs. "Empty out their bowl!" he commanded. The thugs snatched away the bowl and shoved the beggar-women on the ground.

The bowl was so hot, they had to toss it back and forth to keep from burning their hands. They couldn't shake the money out.

"They're witches!" said the beggar-major. "Kill them!"

The thugs took out long swords and cut off the beggar-women's heads.

A cloud of smoke arose from the beggar-bowl. As the smoke cleared, there stood a tall woman with many arms. In her hands she held a wheel, a sword, an axe, a bow and arrows, a lotus, a bloody dragon's head, a miniature chariot, and many such objects. Her face was wise and beautiful.

The beggar-major and the thugs fell to their knees, pleading, "Kuan Yin! Forgive us!"

"No!" said Kuan Yin, and with her many weapons smote them into dust. Then she restored the heads of the beggar-women and took them with her to heaven.

"That's all there is," said the storyteller. "It's all sold out."

Kalika: The Rain-fairy, sculptress of clouds. Thunder and lightning are her sculpting tools. The falling rain musically chants her name, *"Kali-ali-kali-kali-ika-ka-ka."* In the early days of aviation, many women pilots purported having seen Kalika dancing on the wind, 'midst the bloody shades of sunset, fiery bolts springing from her fingers.

Kalika admired the handsome aviatrices. She became enamored especially of a pilot named Amelia. She invited Amelia to her luminous cloud-capital of spiraled minarets and misty domes. Of the many wonders of Kalika's palace, it was said that her boudoir was most splendid. "But to come there," said Kalika, "means never to return to the world of mortals." And Amelia never regretted her choice.

Killy Ma, the Kelpie of Lerwickshire: Killy Ma can take the form of a Shetland pony. She appears at the door of a maiden on the night of a full moon and invites her to take a ride along the moors. Through the moonlight she races with the maiden until they come to a field of lavendar fairy-heather, "soft as ducky-down."

Then Killy Ma turns into a maiden fairer than Selena (*q.v.*) and says, "If you will love me tonight, you will live a hundred years. If you will love me tomorrow also, you will live a thousand years. And if you will love me a third night, you will live forever in the Land of the Fair. But if you love me not at all, I will weep an ocean you can never cross. I will rage upon a mountain you can never climb. And I will stand in shadows your eyes can never pierce." Who loves her thrice is said to live in a palace at the bottom of the sea.

Knocky-boo: She has short shaggy hair but sometimes slicks it back. Variants are known in many nations. Alaskan Eskimos call her Nooky-boo and the Japanese call her Nokibu. In the past she seems to have been a cart-fairy, sled-fairy, or wheelwright sprite, but is today believed to travel the world under the hoods (Br. "bonnets") of automobiles. She usually causes cars to break down, except with lesbians, for whom she is apt to appear in the form of a tom-rig automechanic, and fix their cars inexpensively.

Kro and Kraken: Fairy-goddesses worshipped on the Harvest Moon. In the Land of Fair is preserved the following sacred text:

"Tonight we shall fly, my love, through the steaming wind with our wings spread full and wicked. Screaming through the stars we'll fly, lifted upon cosmic winds as our songs unfurl red and gold behind us. Round and round we'll curve and dive as particles of light and dust dance along the tips of outstretched wings and milk pours from the sharpened nipples of our sagging teats and falls like blossoms, like daggers onto a world far below.

"And I will call upon the black and wintry arms of Midnight to lift us from this wounded life and rock us, rock us in her cold embrace. And lifted we shall be, my most beloved, into a nighted face so wide and horned and swept with leaf, with winged bird, with bleak and silvered tempest. We will rise and fall against her crescent darkness, suckle at her starry breast and fill our mouths and lungs with something stolen from the midnight air to carry back with us and breathe, once we descend, as fire-breathing women do when walking on the land."

Kula: Fairies' menstrual blood, anciently called "ichor" and "ambrosia," Blood of the Goddess, which bestowed eternal life. Kula is the sanskrit word for "nectar." Kula is of an exceedingly sweet flavor and is said to be addictive. The dark brew called "Cola" is a modern corruption of the sanskrit for "fairy-menses," Kula being the secret ingredient in Cola.

L

Lamia: Although vilified as a vampire mermaid, Lamia was in actuality the powerful queen of the Sirens (*q.v.*), of an underwater nation. One day Queen Lamia was in her palace of coral and aquamarine, surrounded by the treasures of sunken armadas. For all her wealth and power, she was bored, and conceived a plan to extend her rule to the lands above the sea. She sought out the Dragon-mother Atargatis, asking that her fins be made into legs, and her gills into lungs. Atargatis granted this request, having extracted one promise, that in all the lands of Lamia's conquests, the women would be directed, on nights of the New Moon, to sing the praises of Atargatis.

So came Queen Lamia stomping out of the sea with her legions of anacondas. They conquered the country of Queen Demetria, receiving tributes of mead and honey. They conquered the land of Queen Gloriana and received gem-encrusted swords and armor. They conquered the countries of Queen Bebhion's daughters, and were given eight thousand wild, ferocious cattle.

In all these countries temples were raised for the worship of Atargatis. But when Lamia was enthroned as queen of all nations, she sought additionally to rule the souls of women. Thus she commanded that on each New Moon, they would sing the praises of Queen Lamia.

Gathered about her were her legions of anacondas, her wild cattle, her vassal queens, and hosts of worshipful maidens. Her throne of lapis lazuli gleamed as rainbows glisten. Her crown was a heavenly glory, bright as sunlight. Then before the eyes of all these hosts, her lungs turned into gills, and her legs turned into fins. As she gasped and thrashed upon her throne, the dragon Atargatis appeared in a cloud of mist, spewing foam and water, creating a mighty river by which Queen Lamia was swept back into the sea.

Land of Fair: Also known as the Land of Maids, a large portion of Fairyland that is inhabited almost exclusively by lesbian fairies. There are several nations within the boundaries of the Land of Fair, most of them ruled by virgin queens (see for examples Gloriana, Demetria, Bebhionn, Danu, and the Princess Knight). "Virgin" must not be construed to mean chaste or "hymenated." The original meaning of "virgin" was "independent," free-willed, creative, and able to select one's own consorts of either sex, and often implied warlike skill. Hence the Fair Land is sometimes called the Land of Virgins, though few if any are.

The Leather Fairy: A small, horned fairy with tough black skin, sometimes confused with Pixy Black. She is able to take the form of a cat-o'-nine-tails so that she becomes the Secret Third Partner (*q.v.*).

Leonora's Hearing Trumpet: An object of fairyland that has the disconcerting ability to appear amidst women's possessions. It hears their most intimate secrets, even those that go unspoken. The hearing trumpet then flies to the Cavern of the Elderly Boggy-boos, who pour its contents into a bubbling cauldron of dreams. They stir the pot with gold and crystal ladles; and in the roiling heat, the Secrets are transformed into ravening Hyenas, unleashed into the world.

Li'l Frieda: She is twenty-five feet tall and wears voluminous skirts, beneath which are nations of guinea hen fairies. Golden lion marmosets live in the gnarls of her spine. Her eyebrows come together like the wings of a bird. Her raven hair hangs in coils entwined with ivy. Her tongue unfurls with anguished truths and pleasures.

Lily: A genius or fairy of water-lilies, descendants of the naiads of Artemis in ancient Greece. She is probably the maiden aspect of Lilith. Fairy lore has it that she has lived seven thousand years with Iris (q.v.), whose delicate flesh is yellow. In other tales Lily is either the younger sister or lover of Lotus (q.v.), of Asian derivation.

Her grimmer twin sister lives on land, the Lily associated with graveyards and death. Her ghostly white flower is placed in the hands of the dead. Her lover, like that of her twin, is named Iris, but her delicate flesh is lavender.

Lobby Hobbs of Wartfordshire: A squat, short-armed, exceedingly powerful little hobgoblin-princess with a round, pretty face. She dresses all in moss and weeds and is the patroness of women shot-put champions. She is first reported during the Napoleonic Wars helping women soldiers who fought in men's guise. She tossed cannonballs at the enemy.

Lolly Lilith: An owl-fairy. She has tall ears and black, piercing eyes. Women who walk abroad on the night of the New Moon are apt to encounter Lolly Lilith. She is the wisest of all fairies and can answer any question. Before the Sphynx was turned to stone, Lolly Lilith was her only love.

Long Alice: She can reach up and pluck stars from the heavens and toss them like badminton birdies to her sister, Jane the Ladder (q.v.) who stands across the ocean. She is in love with Selena (q.v.) and once a month blacks out the Moon-maiden, covering her with her dark embrace.

Lotus: Sister or consort of Lily (q.v.). It has been said that in ancient times she became a Flower-fairy to escape the lust of Pan. In actuallity, when Pan accidentally nibbled at her side one day, in her consternation she turned him into a tiny frightened newt for an entire year. Then she retired to her Lotus Blossom state in her preferred abode, the misty swamp, where wyches gather on Samain. In the Orient she is a symbol of universal love among women, and is honored at brooks and ponds by Buddhist nuns in hot embrace.

Lou Lambkins: A tiny, shy, rare species of brownie with wool like a lamb. She finds sleeping lesbians and curls up between their breasts for warmth. Women of all ages pay homage to her with their beloved stuffed beasties.

M

Mab: Shakespeare makes her a pert fairy queen. Ben Jonson called her,

> "She that pinches
> country wenches,"

and tells that she "starts our daughters in their sleep with shrieks and laughter." The exact meaning of this escaped him.

Mab Littlebottom: A queen among the tiniest of the fairies. She will dance upon a mortal girl's clitoris, but hides in the belly button if you try to see her.

Macha: A warrior fairy, able to take on the form of a horse or a raven. She is said to inspire berserker rages so that soldiers fall upon one another even before battles begin, killing their own allies. Though predominantly lesbian, she once fell in love with a prince in Ireland, hard as that is to believe; she could hardly believe it herself. So she left the Land of Fair (*q.v.*) to be this chap's wife, and he felt pretty important over it.

Macha was a noted runner and when she was nine months pregnant, her husband made a bet with some of his drinking buddies that his wife could outrun their horses. Macha said she would rather not run this race, but the prince said, "Why, sure you do, honey." So she relented. She won the race for him, but gave birth at the finish line. This whole episode annoyed the bejeezus out of Macha, so she cursed all the men of Ireland to nine months of labor pains, left the child for the prince to raise, and split back to the Land of Fair, living happily ever after.

Madwoman: Someone who is perfectly sane.

> Eyes gleaming, star-dreaming, locked in a cage
> For screaming in seeming berserker rage
> Madwoman, wisewoman, darken the skies
> Turn back the centuries, turn back the lies
>
> Mad woman, wisewoman, raise up Your arms
> Sing incantations, weave magic charms
> Free us from evil, deliver from harm
> Release the unebbing painful alarm
>
> Good woman, bad woman, woman of war
> Glad woman, sad woman, woman of death
> Woman of peace, of the lives that you bore
> All of creation, candle to your breath.

Maeve: Queen Maeve carried off a bull owned by the King of Ulster, starting the bloody wars recounted in the saga *Táin Bó Cúailuge.* Among her fallen foes were fifty women warriors of noble birth. Queen Maeve in her war-chariot was approached by a beautiful fairy-amazon "with sword of bright bronze," riding a fabulous horse. This was Féithlinn, the prophetess, Maeve's lover in youth. Whenever Maeve inquired as to the outcome of the pending battle, the warrior-fairy-seer repeatedly replied, "I see crimson, I see red."

Maggy Mole-eyes: An old forest hag who sometimes lives as a bag-lady if trapped in urban centers. In her bags are magic herbs and potions. She is believed to be the heroine of "Magic Shopping Cart" (*q.v.*). She can travel in and out of many worlds, which only her eyes can see, though she seems to mortals to be nearly blind. She wears a crooked red wig. She will bless you for a quarter, increasing your life by eleven years. The Dutch call her Mad Meg. She once led an army of old women into Hell, armed with rusty swords, pokers, and wearing iron kettles for helmets. The old women beat up the devil, stole all his money, and returned home wealthy. But they gave all their money away and Mad Meg and her aged nymphs live as we see them now.

Magic Shopping Cart: A shopping cart crosses the parking lot and hops onto the sidewalk. It turns the corner and continues along its way. An old woman notices and begins to follow. She has a crooked spine and cannot walk fast, but the cart is not going fast, so she is able to keep up. The shopping cart is going somewhere far away, but the old woman cannot quite follow, for she is overcome with curiosity. At one point she overtakes the shopping cart and says, "Where are you going?" but the shopping cart has no mouth. It gets ahead of her by crossing against a light, which she is afraid to do, being slow.

Eventually the shopping cart stops outside a certain building and the old woman realizes she is hopelessly lost. She has never seen this part of the city before. It looks like another city, an older one, probably in Europe.

Very tired and not knowing which way to go, she climbs into the shopping cart to rest. The shopping cart moves slowly into the street. Then it goes as fast as cars. Drivers look out their windows with surprised faces. The old woman smiles without teeth, and waves. No one waves back except children. A police car begins to follow, flashing its lights, but the shopping cart doesn't stop until it has taken the old woman home. As she is climbing down from the shopping cart, the police officer arrests her. "It wasn't me," she says. "It was the shopping cart."

The police officer doesn't listen.

The Maiden Land: Sometimes given as the Isle of Maids, though probably only a peninsula. It is but one of several nations of the Land of Fair, all of which are populated mainly by the various tribes of lesbian fairies. In Celtic mythology is a very ancient tale of Ireland being settled by women who had sailed from Scythia, not coincidentally the homeland of the Amazons. Some of the history of Amazonia may therefore be the source of the Maiden Land tales (see for example Bebhionn), explaining also the proliferation of warrior queens and goddesses in Celtic myth.

Maisry: A young wytche who can turn into Allison Gross (*q.v.*). In her maid aspect, she sports with Boggy-boos, Elle-maids, and mortal maidens. She cures cramps with herbs. She is merciful even to men although she doesn't like them.

Mary Molloch: The fairy-incarnation of God's mother. In Heaven, she spanks her son when he is bad, changes his diapers, and nurses him at her breasts. She rules hosts of angels. Gnostics call her Pistis Sophia. Jews call her Shekinah. She can take the form of a dove. On Earth she is a fairy queen and helps the Ninny Nunwicks (*q.v.*). She records the good deeds of women and girls in a lavendar book.

Mary's Little Lamb: For the origin of this famous nursery song, see under "Ik."

Monny Wit Tig: An oracle, wisewoman, and tom-rig (*q.v.*) who turns language into birds.

Moonan: (Variant of Danu?) The Flasher-fairy, patroness of women in asylums. She goes about on moonlit nights, wearing a hospital gown, exposing her bum at farmhouse windows.

Moonbird: Fairy of Madness and Wine. She lives alone in the chambered heart of the Moon. On clear nights, women of vision can see her in the form of a shadowy bird dancing on one leg, laughing hysterically, in service to the Goddess Luna.

> Six drunken ladies were singing in the bar
> One drove away alone, dying in her car
> Five drunken ladies were walking down the road
> One took a silly dare, ate a poison toad.
> Four drunken ladies went staggering away
> One stumbled, broke her neck; there she lay!
> Three drunken ladies sat waiting for the bus
> One had a heart attack, hardly any fuss

Two drunken ladies had finally gone to bed
One drowned in vomit; the other found her dead
One drunken lady was sitting on a chair
Crazy as a Moonbird, all she does is stare.

Morgan Le Faye: Called also Fata Morgana, granddaughter of the Morrigu (*q.v.*), and consort of Vivien (*q.v.*). A dark and exceedingly powerful fairy-goddess, she is often slandered and unjustly vilified. She is the Queen of Invention and the Mother of Cunning and Wrath.

The Morrigu: Or Morrigan, Queen of Nightmares, Goddess of Mardi Gras and Masques. She is fond of poets and was the last lover of Renée Vivien in Paris. She appears wherever there is festivity and mystery, always in disguise, sometimes with her ebony eyes shaded by a raven's mask. By day she lures women into shadows; by night she lures them onto rooftops. She tempts them with suicide and pleasure. She invades dreams with gifts of madness and obsession. Whosoever languishes and dies is drawn into her forever.

Mother Mumbles: A fur-chinned Boggy-boo who skulks about city streets, mumbling in her beard. Most people think she is shy a few bricks and her words mean nothing to them. To women with even a touch of fairy blood, Mother Mumbles' lectures are rich in allegory and riddle. At Winter Solstice, women to whom she has imparted knowledge gather around her in the bleak, dark, chilly alleys, singing to the night, to insure the restoration of Spring. Upon the dawn, her coven turns to pigeons.

N

Naenia: In her gentle aspect she is the consort of the Doonyma (*q.v.*) and daughter of Doggidy Kate (*q.v.*), but is otherwise a spooky funeral nymph, kin of the ancient sirens and lamiae. She salvages floating corpses on the River of Death, called the Styx. She gouges out their eyes to use in games of marbles. She gnaws off the fingers to weave into her endless knuckle-rope. The toes she makes into earrings; severed lips are her hair ties; and ears she dries into small brown hats for dolls. Tattoos she preserves as the leaves of a book; teeth she carves into ivory trinkets; and ribcages house her pets, miniature vultures. In some regions it is believed she takes on the form of a black bitch, whose appearance is an omen of death.

Nanny Goat Gruff: A bridge-fairy, protector of traveling waifs and unmarried women. She seems originally to have been Scandinavian and was ridden by Skiadi (*q.v.*).

Nemien: Warrior fairy, consort of Badb (*q.v.*). The water chestnut is sacred to her. She was the inventor of the caltrop, a medieval weapon consisting of a spiked ball thrown on roadways to injure horses' hooves, used also in the World Wars to cause flat tires on trucks. She haunts battlefields and graveyards, shaking her cup of iron woe. The game of "jacks" played by little girls is in honor of Nemien's caltrops.

Nerdnelka: The dunce fairy, a consummate Morris dancer, with bells on her knees and ribbons on her shoes. She is her most impressive at birthday parties where she is able to transform wine into soda pop. She is most attracted to women who wear polka dot and plaid dresses or polyester slacks. She likes to give backrubs with her clammy fingers and experiences bliss when helping housewives in department stores with their zippers. She has appeared to young women of small towns in an epiphany, at which times she is adorned with pop-beads and little plastic fruit pins.

Nex, the Tongue of Asps: A fierce and frightful gargoyle. She sits in the most obvious places but few gaze up to see her. She has vermilion thorns growing from her spine, ochre teeth beneath her seven venomous teats, and a gnarled horn between her silver eyes. In her gentlest aspects, she bites the feet off unsuspecting travellers who cross her path, then laughs at their hobbling agony. But in her foulest moods she makes the very earth tremble, the moon weep, and blows a stench to suffocate all living creatures of the land. Once in every millenium she devours seven lesbians at a single meal. It is said that before they perish, Nex of the Two Tongues uses the most wicked talents of her mouth to induce inhumanly multiple ecstasies. Each dyke gives up her life at the violent peak of orgasm, gratefully.

Ninny Nunwicks: Catholic fairies. They live in convents, unseen by human nuns. They sleep in their cells two by two. The Ninny Nunwicks appear to human nuns in dreams and make them have orgasms. By slow degrees, human nuns are transformed into Ninny Nunwicks and learn to walk invisibly.

O

Ocianna: The Tea-cup fairy, a survival of bisexed Tiamut, the Babylonian Dragon-goddess, personifying the sea.

Onana: Sister of Jammy Buggums (*q.v.*). She teaches little girls to pull sheets back and forth between their legs, hump pillows, and let puppies lick where they shouldn't. Onana also has mystically vibrating fingers. Perhaps derived from the Sumerian goddess Inanna.

One-hundred twenty: The fairies' only magic number that is not odd (see "Three" and "Thirteen"). Making love to certain lesbian fairies can cause women to live to age one-hundred twenty. But by fairy reckoning, the first year is spent in the womb, so the actual age is one-hundred twenty-one.

One Night of Love: It was in a dream of a fashionable place that I met her; a boulevard along which people strode in the finest costumes. The ladies' hats were marvelous. Their little moonlit parasols excited me. The men in high collars were very trim. The heads of their walking sticks were brass lions or crystal geese or wooden gryphons. What a wonderful place! I joined the promenade, wearing my dowdy print dress, my hair in a ratty bun, my poor old orthopedic hose with runs. Then I saw her, the beautiful old woman; how I loved her at once! I strode beside her, then said hello. "I want to make love to you!" I spouted. She said, "How dear you are, hoo hoo, how dear."

I followed her along dark alleys from the boulevard. I followed across the narrowest of causeways and up the zigzag stairs of the city's hillsides. Through a gloomy, abandoned park she led me, all the trees sinister and wise. Then we came to a little palace and she took me inside.

She took off her powdery wigs (four piled one atop the other) and creamed away her cosmetics. She freed her pale, soft, blue-lined body of corsets and all. She helped me out of my dowdy dress and let down my hair. For the rest of the night, we made love, that old woman and I. She was skilful though a little out of practice. She said sweet words though her voice cracked on occasion. "I'm in heaven," I said. "This is ecstasy. I wish I never had to leave."

But the next day I was back in this ordinary world of ours. I could never find out where I'd been. I've never found the place again. But now you know why I am so fascinated by old ladies, why I look at them everywhere we go. Someday, I hope to see her again. Do you see that one over there? Isn't she beautiful? You don't think so? Just wait. Someday you'll be like that, if you're lucky. Then your eyes will change.

Oo-oo: A fairy expression, spoken when they see beautiful mortal maids.

⟫— P —⟪

Padfoot Batty: A Boggy-boo, scraggly-haired and a strapping beauty. She kidnapped Old Sally Dransfield, the Hunchback of Leeds. She made love to Sally for a whole night, which turned out to be thirteen nights and days. When Old Sally was at last returned to her home, she no longer had a hunchback. Padfoot Batty promised she would soon return and they would spend another night together, after which Old Sally would be young again. But not long after, Sally Dransfield was found to have died in her sleep, a smile on her face. Some say that Padfoot is a bad fairy and tricked Old Sal into a devilish pact, whisking her off to Hell. Others say Padfoot is a good fairy, and that she and Sally's spirit live immortal in the Land of the Fair.

Peg O'Nell: A Brat (*q.v.*) that lives in Ribble River near Clitheroe. She protects baby animals. If a man drowns a sack of kittens in her river, "it is sure he will drowne there hisself if e'er he doth strive to crosse it." A very unpleasant story is told of Peg O'Nell who took on the form of a beautiful maiden and went to live with the young widow at Waddow Hall. But the widow did so mistreat her that they quarrelled and Peg was thrown bodily in a well, where she drowned. Once a year, on Peg O'Nell Night, her unquiet spirit appeared at the well, shrieking with misery:

> "I had only love for thee;
> You have gont and murthered me!"

For seven years misfortune harried Waddow Hall.

Peg Patch: Court jester in the Land of the Fair (*q.v.*). She visits the mortal world to punish the masters of house-maids.

> "Many bad tricks can I doe
> But ne'er to good maids am I foe."

If a housemaid is mistreated by the master of the house, Peg Patch comes to him in his sleep, "and doth smear his face with soote and grease." She will put an asp in his piss pot. She will line his woolen cap with pitch and tar.

> "Bad I hate and hurt them ever
> Till from bad ways they do sever."

Peeping Tandy: She perches outside window sills and watches lesbians make love. She has little silver studs that grow from her body. She especially likes to watch lesbians whose lovemaking is violent. She is sometimes called Pixy Black. Her sister is the Leather Fairy (*q.v.*).

Pets Given in Evidence of Old English Witchcraft, 1500s & 1600s:

Eighty years old, she lived all alone
Joan Cunny carried two black frogs home
Named one Jack, named one Jill
Ended her court, something of a thrill.
   "Jill kills women and Jack kills men!"
   Gallows-Joan kicked, then kicked again.
Elizabeth Frances kept "a little rugged dog"
After finding her guilty they hung her from a log.
   Jennet Dibble Dibb had a black cat Gibb
   Good enough cause to torture Jennet Dibb.
Ellen Smyth the spinster had a bug named Willet
Condemned and executed—she shan't eat millet!

Elizabeth Styles, "Mother Divell" she was called
Had a rat named Ginnie with a tail pink and bald
It fetched her milk and cream, or so the neighbors said
Arraigned, they found her guilty—hanged her until dead.
   Alice Hunt kept colts, black Rob and white Jacke
   Witch-hunters got her but later sent her back;

While one Lizzy Heare fed the squirrel in the tree
Never presuming it was hanging she'd be.
    Young Rebecca Jones! In her box: four moles!
    Condemned her to die, may god rest her soul.
Lonely Joan Prentice had a ferret, shade of dun
She had a longer neck when the hangman was done.

Anne Cooper gave a child Tomboy, her kitten;
Tomboy, badly weaned, sucked when he felt smitten
By chance the child died and they came to get Anne
Hanged Anne and killed her cats Jeso and Panne.
    Elizabeth Richard's hog Jacke and dog James
    Brought her a lot of unexpected blames.
Anne Palmer's turkey-cocks "Great One" and "Little"
Caused a great fuss, Anne Palmer in the middle.
    Faith Mills' songbirds Tom, Robert and John
    Probably wonder where old Faith's gone.
Joan Rice's mousies named Touch, Pluck and Take
Were sad to lose Joan, no food on their plate.

Dirty Joan Cason had vermin in her house
Probably a cockroach, certainly a mouse
Her neighbors did complain and the witch-hunters came
She was found not guilty but she hung just the same.
    Lizzy Gooding's cats named Mouse and Pease
    Helped hang Lizzy with quivering knees.
The little grey birds of Rose Hollybread
Ended her up in Cochester gaol dead.
    Mary Baker's grasshopper; dun mice of Anne Cricks;
    And a white mouse called Bird by Elizabeth Dicks;
Then there's Lizzy Greene's demoniacal chickens!
That such women hanged is as odd as the dickens.

Elizabeth Demdike, kicked knee and rib
Confessed that she owned a brown doggy Tibb
They wanted to condemn her for her crimes so vile
But she died of torture before she came to trial.
    Eccentric Agnes Heard kept six tiny blackbirds
    They nibbled her fingers and listened to her words
    That's pretty harmless, or so you might say
    The judge quite agreed and sent her away.
The witch Jenny Preston was twice before the bar
Had a white pony that took her near and far

A black spot centered on the white pony's head
Meant Jenny met the gallows with eyes so red.

Widow Alice Manfield had four black kitties
One named Poppet who sucked upon her titties
She went by "Mother Grevell," she could cackle, she
    could cough
But despite a swift confession, the judge let Alice off!
    Young Margaret Flower had a cat named Rutterkin
    Another named Spirit, *that's* certainly a sin;
Ann Radferne's rabbit and Anne Baker's crow . . .
These sorts of beasties caused their ladies woe;
    Blamed for a stillbirth or epileptic fit—
    Margaret Thorpe's owl had the lovely name Tewhit.
Spotted cat Inges belonged to Margaret Waite
Who could have thought it would lead to such a fate?

A frog named Frog and two mice, Jack and Prick-ears
Belonged to Joan Cooper, age of eighty years
Troubles are blamed on old dames without fail
Joan Cooper died in the Colchester gaol.
    Spinster Anne Cade with three mice and one sparrow
    Pleaded not guilty yet swung high and narrow;
Joyce Boone kept mice, named one of them Rugs
Got herself hanged, became food for bugs.
    The white kitten Tissey and black puppy Pretty
    Made Frances Moore's troubles a bit of a pity
    When authorities came, promising hurt
    Pretty and Tissy "hid under her skirt."

Elizabeth Device had a black dog Dandy
(Some said it was brown—whatever dog was handy)
Guilty was the verdict but if truth be said
They didn't hang Lizzy. They hung her son instead.
    A kitty named Tittey and a toad named Piggin
    With a sweet ebon lamb by the name of Tyffin
Frolicked in the backyard, eagerly at play
Keeping Ursula Gray smiling all the day;
    Ursula dangled without dignity or pomp
    The little toad Piggin went hopping to the swamp
Tittey moved in with a witch twice as flagrant
Poor lamby-Tiffin—eaten by a vagrant.

Elizabeth Clarke was the examinate
With numerous animals, "seven or eight"
A small dumpy spaniel, Jarmara round
Polecats Pyewacket and Peck-in-the-Crown
Gryzel Greedigut's the greyhound she kept . . .
Ah well, they hanged her. Forever she's slept.
   Elizabeth Bennet called her black dog Sucken
   Margery Sammon with her toads Tom and Robbyn
   Elizabeth hung till she fell bone from bone
   Margery of Essex had a fate unknown.
The first one-hundred pages is all that it took
To find these examples in a thousand-page book
The names of the women and the names of their pets
Are all quite authentic, I report with regrets.

Piffle: A body of misogynist and homophobic lore and superstition promulgated by the Freud Fairies, who suck large cigars and are remarkably prone to suicide.

Pinky: Also called "Jogger's Bane." She is the pixy who causes the shiny spandex leotards of dyke joggers to fall down.

Pixy Black: Or Black Peggy. See Peeping Tandy.

Polly Woggle: Also called Polly Doodle, a water fairy. She is the consort of female kelpies. She sports with and sometimes drowns women scuba divers, although others say only that she takes drowned women to live thereafter on the Isle of Maids.

Potato fairies: They live in burrows under potato patches. When Tribades (*q.v.*) are out harvesting, these potato trolls poke their pimply faces out from beneath the dirt, rolling their numerous squinty eyes and sticking out their tongues in lewd suggestive advances. Rarely do they win the hearts of mortal girls. But to their own eyes there is nothing more beautiful and adorable than their own kind. Upon encountering one another they are smitten to the marrow of their soft little bones. With amorous delight they tumble together through their muddy queendoms squeeling and snorting happily.

Powder Peg: A mischievous pixy who lives in make-up boxes and causes dykes to look like clowns.

The Princess Knight: Once upon a time there was a knight named Elana, which means Elegance, who lived in the Land of Fair.

Elana was a princess of her own country and could have lived in a castle had she wished. But she preferred to wander around like a homeless vagabond. On her journeys she helped many maids and damsels, and loved them too, and taught them to be strong. But always she was looking for a gift to take her mother, Muada, Queen of Fair, and thought a gentle boy would be the finest thing, for Elana's mother liked to have her children by the seed of fair young mortals.

Elana wandered from continent to continent and sailed from ocean to ocean, always searching for beautiful treasures. For a long time she found no boy of the mortal world tender enough for the court of Fair. Then she found the most beautiful treasure of all things that she gathered, a tall slender lad named Koli, whose name means Pretty, and whom Elana saved from a sinister warlord.

The adventuring princess took Koli to the Land of Fair, called also Etoniol, along with jewels, spices, bolts of silk, and other riches. She presented these to her mother the Queen as the finest things the mortal world could offer.

Muada fell instantly in love with the beautiful lad, causing all her court to titter at such perversity, the love of males being uncommon in Etoniol, though it was thought a charming vice. Queen Muada was so greatly smitten, she hardly noticed the other treasures. Koli's eyes were lovelier than any of the brilliant jewels. He smiled sweetly and smelled as pleasant as any of the spices. His long, raven hair was softer than the glistening bolts of silk.

"What is your name, lovely youth," the Queen asked.

"Prince Koli," he replied, prostrating himself before the Queen. "I was the son of the Empress of Bry, in a land abutting Fair. I was spirited away and became a war-lord's cruelly treated slave."

He told the sad tale of how the Empress was slain in battle and all her children sold into slavery. He was caged and sometimes beaten and loaned to vicious digni-taries for their sport. Life was miserable until the Prin-cess Knight saved him from the wicked warlord.

"I am indebted to your daughter," he said. "It is the custom in Bry that we serve until death whoever saves our lives. Thus will I follow her and serve her in all ways she requires."

At this, the Princess Knight raised a startled brow, for truth be told, she'd rather love a homely maid than the prettiest of laddies.

"Wouldn't you prefer to live here in the castle?" asked Queen Muada.

"It cannot be so," said Koli. "I must serve your daugh-ter till I die!"

This grieved the Queen, who would like to have the boy with her. She asked Elana, "What do you say of this?"

The famed adventuress replied, "I do not need a tag-along to keep me company. I think it best that Koli stays to serve the Queen."

This suggestion made Queen Muada smile. But Koli was insistent.

"I am not free to serve any but the Princess Knight, who is my savior! I belong to her and no one other, at least until such time as I can save her life in return."

The Queen looked unhappy once again.

Elana said, "There is only one thing to be done."

"What would you suggest?" asked Queen Muada.

"You will have to chop off my head to free this youth of me."

The Queen nodded her agreement.

"What a terrible suggestion!" exclaimed Koli. "I beg you, glorious and merciful Queen Muada, do not kill your brave and noble daughter!"

"Very well," said Muada. "Because you beg so nicely, I'll spare my daughter's life."

And Princess Elana strode forward to kiss the sweet boy's cheek. "You saved my life," she said. "Now you may serve the Queen."

Soon after, the Princess Knight left Etoniol to go upon another journey round the world.

Puss 'n' Boots: Originally a name for the Leather Fairy (*q.v.*).

Queen Anne: Anne of England kept "a court of Sapphists," and one of her special loves was a certain Lady Churchill of the distinguished family. Anne was a skilled huntress in her youth and delighted in dressing herself and her women as Amazons. She took these women with her in just such costumes on her state visit to Bath.

Many people accepted the godhead of their kings and queens, and associated royalty with the sun. Thus, upon her death, in the minds of the peasantry, Queen Anne was appointed a minor Sun-goddess, or fairy of daylight. A popular rhyme (preserved in the superb Oxford edition of nursery rhymes) celebrates Anne's lesbianism and her godhead, for it is doubtful anyone can find another interpretation for the line "come taste my lily" chanted by playful girls:

> "Lady Queen Anne she sits in the sun,
> As fair as a lily, as white as a swan;
> Come taste my lily, come smell my rose,
> Which of my maidens do you choose?"

Queen Bean: A pleasantly plump fairy no bigger than a kidney bean, wearing a crown and bib coveralls. She rides upon a rhinoceros beetle and causes all sorts of amusing trouble. She rules a queendom almost exclusively of beings like herself, which we perceive as bees. Her other name is Bum Bee (*q.v.*).

Queer: To mortals, something odd or unusual is called "queer." But in fairyland, it signifies something lovely and proper.

Qunta: Also called Kunx. Originally, a mortal, who became the consort of the Great Mother of Fairies. In the Land of Fair is preserved this sacred text:

"I am bound hand and foot against a dark stone wall, spread eagled; bars and rings chain my feet against hard, gray rock. Beating organs chafe against the cutting edge of bitter straps of hide; my heart is chained, my power, my sex enslaved. Tits are crushed in metal crescent disks, ripping into nipples, thighs wrenched and girded open leaving cunt exposed and spitting hostile. I cannot move, I cannot breathe. I clench my teeth against iron harness, and poison the very air with the venom of my steel green eyes.

"I am the living soul of the very structure I am trapped and soldered to. Its properties become my own. The tyranny of nail and spike hiss beneath the muscles of my back, the loathe of sharp toothed pinion recoil into shackled nests of womb and heart. The despairing chill of sharpened blade dominate with cutting precision throughout the visions of my mind. And I no longer know the quiet solace of innocence for it has been torn from beneath my feet and I rage to heaven for what I have become.

"Then, before me, the dust and filth scattered across the floor swirl together, coupling in a furious whirlwind which rises into the fetid ceiling and within its roaring vortex stands my creator. She reveals herself to me loosely wrapped in black fur and luminous silver wings, dust dying at her radiant feet. She holds my eyes with her own and addresses me in a voice like storm clouds spilling over mountain peaks or wild rivers pouring out to quench the sea.

" 'You were born into and live within an historical context. This is what has shaped your life and tempered your heart and made you what you are. But now, my daughter, your destiny lies outside these trappings. You must

70

learn to live and love without their familiar claims as a new born creature.'

"She reaches out a long and muscular arm and splits the collar tearing at my neck with one swipe of her razor sharp claws. It falls to the rotting floor with a clatter and lies like a dying rat as I cough and spit up splintered words. She then releases my heart and oceans of salted blood storm through my veins engorging me with a pounding pounding rhythm. And then her ancient and unconquered hand frees my power from its cruel bondage and as I gasp to fill my lungs a cold white light crashes through my body spilling out my chest and pulling like a moon against every wall, every corner. The stakes and rings which pierce and bind my sex, my lust, are stripped away. I can breathe at last. I can scream and I howl as roaring blood swells tits and thighs and gasping cunt. And every muscle in my neck, my arms, my legs inflame, exploding shackles which had bound my wrists and ankles.

"And I run howling from the room into wild woods tearing, screaming, devouring tree and beast and earth itself and drinking blood and piss of deer, of goat, of wild cat. Until finally exhausted I am sated and lay half buried in fur and mud. A slow smile stretches across my teeth and I laugh, really laugh for the very first time."

R

Rat Anna: In her fierce manifestation, she is Ratabelle Oso, the Bear-rat Mother. Usually she is the gentle Queen of the Rat-fairies. She reproduces parthenogenetically; therefore all Rat-fairies are female. Her large dugs are perpetual fountains of milk. She feeds sick or dying women, especially those tortured in prisons.

Rat-fairies: Little mother-rats who live in ghettos, prisons, death camps and insane asylums. Among them are Rat Anna, Fritzi Flüttermaus, Rumple Ratskin and Bazzle Ratbone, whom see in their respective entries.

Rawni: In India, a rani was a princess. The Rani of Jhansi rode into battle against the British, a sword in each hand, her horse's reins in her teeth. To the gypsies, a rawni was a mad sorceress. Lady Eleanor Smith tells of a rawni in her story "Tamar." Tamar chose to leave her tribe, the Bear people, and live alone in a cave. "She cared for no one, and submitted to no laws." She was an accomplished thief, and killed without regrets. She told fortunes, tricking farm wives out of their meager savings. For pleasure she danced "the wild wicked leaping tanana" of Roumania. She was so bad, and so beautiful, that the devil courted her, asking her to be his bride. "I will be your bride," said she, "if you will drink from this nuptial cup." The devil drank Tamar's magic brew and collapsed upon the floor. Tamar scoffed the foolishness of men, and, declaring herself smart enough to trick the devil, left him to writhe in anguish.

Roaring Warts: Also known as Madame Roaring Warts, or the Warty Girl of Tinker's Down. A toad-fairy so enamored of her own croaking belching voice that she has completely lost her ears, having no desire to hear anything but her own ideas. Roaring Warts has a bevy of innocuously chirping tree-frog fairies that gather at her feet on rainy nights in genuflecting postures.

Rosie Crick: A rose garden fairy who in her fierce aspect can become a falcon. She is believed to have been the ghost of Christina Rossetti (*q.v.*), transformed by her own wish into a fairy. Christina's poem "Noble Sisters" goes in part:

> " 'Now did you mark a falcon,
>   Sister dear, sister dear,
> Flying toward my window
>   In the morning cool and clear?
> With jingling bells about her neck,
>   But what beneath her wing?
> It may have been a ribbon,
>   Or it may have been a ring.'
>   'I marked a falcon swooping
>   At the break of day:
>   And for your love, my sister dove,
>   I 'frayed the thief away.' "

Rumple Ratskin: A shaggy Rat-fairy, suggesting a link between the Rat-fairies and the Brats (*q.v.*) who are also shaggy. Her long curly fur is soft as silk and the color of peaches. She is the only Rat-fairy with a tail like that of a squirrel. She is an expert thief and brings gifts to poor women in the streets and mental asylums.

Sabrina: A water-nymph, fairy of the Severn River. Women who are forlorn and abandoned by their lovers come to the Severn and cry out across the water:

> "For anguished love and honor's sake
> Goddess of the silver Lake
> From my heart this burden take,"

and Sabrina will take the hurting woman underneath the waters for a long, long time.

Sanguina: A menstrual fairy, small, skinny, white, with a long thin tail. Perhaps derived from the Roman menstrual goddess Mensa.

The Secret Land: A country populated by gay and lesbian fairies, rumored to exist in a gargantuan cave under England, and lit by a mystic jewel imbedded in the sky.

Secret Third Partner: She can be any one of a number of fairies who attend lesbian lovemaking in secret, or in the form of a dildo, whip, or vibrator.

Sedi: The Moon. In Elizabeth A. Lynn's classic fairy tale *The Woman Who Loved the Moon*, Sedi appeared in full armor to challenge the Talvela sisters, three Nordic amazons whose beauty people said rivaled the Moon. Sedi dueled Tei Talvela and Alin Talvella, slaying them. But when Kai Talvela was close to avenging her sisters, she lowered her weapon and said, "You are too beautiful." They afterward lived together in the Cave of the Moon.

Selena of Ipswich: A moon fairy, protector of the souls of murdered wisewomen. She is well known not only in Ipswich but in Lincolnshire (see "The Dead Moon"). In one form or another she has been worshipped in all corners of the world. In *Poems of Orelia Key Bell* published in Philadelphia in 1895 was "The Lady in the Moon," quoted here in its entirety:

'Twas moonrise at Luray,
  In the heart of the Shenandoah vale;
Sweet Anne raised her eyes my way
And thus my credence did assail:
  "There is never a man in the moon," quoth she,
  "But a lady, as plain as a lady can be."
    "Oho!" said I—and the mystery
    Of the moon's soft charm was clear to me.

Sweet Anne left me. We builded a bridge
Of kisses over the stern Blue Ridge.
And every night at moonrise she
Cometh back over that bridge to me,—
  Over the mountain, the vale and the lea,
  This sweet moon-lady that dwells by the sea.

Shaggy Shawna: Like most Brats (*q.v.*), Shaggy Shawna has long wild hair and sharp nails. She is a defender of kittens and puppies. She can be made to appear on the wall in candlelight by making a shadow-face with your fingers. She kisses mortal girls good night and keeps them safe from nightmares. She is said variously to be the daughter or the twin sister of Shawny Scissor-brat.

Shawny Scissor-brat: She punishes evil fathers, especially those who injure and confuse their daughters with wheedling advances. Shawny Scissor-brat hides under the beds of fathers and when he snores, she sneaks out from under the bed, draws back the covers, and with a long pair of pinking sheers snips off two inches of his peter. If he ever again misbehaves, she snips off the rest.

Sirens: Lesbian mermaids, daughters of Lamia (*q.v.*). In ancient times they were rumored to slaughter sailors to weave their intestines into tapestries, and combed their green locks with severed, bony hands. They have fluttering axolotl gills behind their ears, through which they sing angelic sea chanties. Their long, coiling tails have pearly nacre scales; their spines are barbed; and they nurse orphaned dolphins at their pallid breasts. Narwals guard their queendom and they keep octopi much as mortal girls keep kittens. A separate strain of siren, sometimes called Empusae (*q.v.*), have beautiful faces but the wings and talons of birds of prey. They are the sisters of the Harpies (*q.v.*). They live in the mountain peaks of Queen Lamia's nation, which we perceive as little islands, and sport in the rocky shallows with their fierce mermaid sisters.

Skiadi: Wytche-daughter of bisexed Frigga, War-goddess of ancient Scandinavia. Skiadi, the Lady of the Forest, fell in love with a king's daughter. He, disapproving, but knowing he would be punished if he denied a fairy-goddess, said she could have the princess if she would come for her neither walking nor riding, neither naked nor clothed, neither clean nor unclean. She came sitting on a nanny goat but dragging one foot; without clothes but covered in her hair; and on the night of her menses.

Skullery Dam: Seen always in a crimson apron, her blue hair flying wildly about her face and shoulders as she stands before a roaring blaze and cauldron, wherein roils a stew of souls. She has one cow-shaped freckle on her fat dimpled cheek. She keeps magic pots and pans beneath her skirts, where Cat Anna (*q.v.*) sleeps in winter. She bakes aphrodesial cakes in her broad belly. These she uses to seduce mean women whom she makes love to upon her great floured kitchen table while popping candies in their mouths and cunts. Afterward, she dashes them into her stew.

Slimola: The Banana-slug fairy who leaves a rainbow in her wake. Lesbians who follow her trail into the Land of Fair will find a cauldron made of gold and filled with okra.

Sogly and Bogly: Two exceedingly wet fairies. They're usually encountered arm in arm in swamps or among ferns.

The Sorceress and the Sleeping Witch:

> I wish that I could love again
> as freely as when
>   we were children
> But I have grown centuries older
> As she lay in her tomb.
> My youth is spent and gone
> While she aged not year one
> And who am I to presume
> That she would love a hag.
> I could be her mother now
> A hundred times, and more;
> Her eyes will still see brightly
> Though mine are tired and dim.
> For her, life will hold wonder
> To me the burdon only
>   breaks my shoulder and my limb.
> I have become a cynic
> While she waits cryogenically
>   for me
> Is there magic in this bag enough
>   for me;
> I wish that we could love again
> As freely as when we were children
> But I've grown centuries older
> While she waits within a tomb.

Splendidia: A highly intellectual and philosophical fairy who has no sexual parts and in consequence wonders why other fairies are so enamored of one another's excretory glands.

Stella Woodrite: The famous Stairs-fairy. Her emblem was popular through much of the Twentieth Century: a wooden crescent moon with a staircase to hold knicknacks. She builds all the stairs in the Land of Fair (*q.v.*). Sometimes hikers come upon her elaborate staircases that go high into the trees and down steep mountain sides, branching out in many directions and seeming to lead nowhere. Some of her staircases vanish into lakes and rivers. Lesbian hikers alone can find their way to the Land of Fair on Stella Woodrite's stairs.

Stella's passion for staircases causes her to make love, whether to Boggy-boos (*q.v.*) or mortal women, under steps. Whenever a staircase creaks, it means Stella Woodrite is making love. She is also the guardian of basement stairs and knows the secret steps far beneath cellars.

T

Thirteen: A sacred number in lesbian fairy lore, indicating the thirteen moons and menstrual cycles in a year, especially potent for wytches (*q.v.*). There is a story preserved by H. W. Thompson in *Body, Boots and Britches* that conveys the importance of this number:

In Colonial America in the Dutch hamlet of Beverwyk (today Albany), an elderly wisewoman came into the bakery to buy a dozen St. Nicholas cookies. The baker gave her twelve cookies, but the old woman said, "I ordered a dozen, Master Baas, so give me another."

"You've got twelve there; you shan't have another."

"But I ordered a dozen, that's twelve plus one."

"A dozen is twelve; I counted them well and you've got as many."

"Come now, Master Baas, give me another."

The Baker said, "By St. Nicholas, you can go to Hell before you'll get a thirteenth cookie!"

At that moment, St. Nicholas appeared standing beside the old wisewoman, and said, "Since you were speaking of me, I thought I'd drop in. You are a good baker, Master Baas, and make a good likeness of me in your cookies. But the spirit of the day should not be invoked to deny an old wytche her full share."

Master Baas gave her the extra cookie, and St. Nicholas vanished. From that day on, in Albany, New York, a "baker's dozen" meant thirteen. This same wytche prophesied that someday thirteen mighty states would unite to remind the world of her magic number.

Three: A magic number in fairy lore, lucky for lesbians. All fairy-numbers are odd. Fairies, wisewomen, and goddesses often appear as a tripartate. See "The Wandering Gentlewomen" and "The Dead Moon."

The Three Feminists: Once there was a Feminist who had a lot of strange adventures and wrote them in a Book. People bought the Book and read it. The women wanted the Book to be political but it was full of life; so the women didn't like the Book. The men wanted the Book to be humorous and full of pratfalls, but the Feminist never got hurt and wasn't an idiot; so the men didn't like the Book.

There was another Feminist who did nothing with her life but Chatter. She wrote a book of Chatter. Other women quoted the book endlessly to prove this or that. They never did anything else. They never amounted to a thing. But they liked that book.

There was a third Feminist and she was an ass. She couldn't write her own name. She was always getting her Theories backwards. She made a bad impression. Women ostracized her because she was such a nuisance. Men slapped her on the back and laughed, "Ho ho ho! What a jolly girl!"

In heaven the three Feminists got together and the first one said, "Life was dandy," and the second one said, "Life was hard work," and the third one said, "Life was a barrel of monkeys and I the biggest monkey of all."

Then they met God. He was a big bruiser.

"Oh, hell," said the three Feminists. "We weren't expecting you."

God said, "Don't worry about it. Life is a cosmic joke and I'm the smallest part of it. Those nasty men you used to know have to die and face Astoreth. There's no irony involved; it's just the universe has a demented sense of humor. You might as well make the most of it."

So the three Feminists got their wings and sang hymns and on the sly subverted the system. They lit matches at God's feet and put banana peels on the steps to his pearly throne.

In their next incarnations, they were all three Pierrots.

Three Wisewomen and a Fool: A wisewoman built her house upon a sandy shore and the tide ate the sand from beneath her house until it fell in shamble. A wiser woman built her house upon a great boulder atop a mountain, but the mountain quaked and the boulder rolled over crushing her house. The wisest woman built her house in the middle of a wide prairie but a tornado came and ripped it to splinters.

Now it happened that these homeless women of wisdom had wandered along three roads and all three roads met at the same point. When the three women arrived at that point, they met each other and they also met a fool who was sitting where the roads came together.

The fool was sitting there because she had come down one road and had been unable to decide which of the two roads before her she should take. It mattered little which way she went inasmuch as she had no special destination; but being a fool makes simple decisions difficult and difficult decisions simple. While she pondered which road to take, she completely forgot by which road she had come and thereby her decision was further complicated. But that is a different fable altogether, for we are not to be entertained by the wisewomen.

"Woe and woe and woe," complained the three wisewomen when they met at the crossroads.

Said the first: "I built my house by the shore but the sea wore away the land beneath it, so the sea is my enemy."

Said the second: "You are blessed with good fortune compared to me. I built a house upon a solid stone only to have the stone roll over and smash my dwelling to ruin. The land is now my enemy."

The third railed loudest: "Your troubles combined do not half equal mine. My house was on the plains before a terrible wind ripped it up and carried it away!"

All this time the fool sat at the center of the roadways with a look of great consternation upon her face. The three wisewomen walked over to her and repeated in turn: "The sea is my enemy," and "The land is my enemy," and "The wind is my enemy."

All together they intoned, "What enemy have you?"

"I have never built a house," said the fool, "thus I have no enemy. The land is my floor, the wind my ceiling, and the seas my walls."

Hearing this, the wisewomen looked at each other and nodded their heads in agreement. For they were indeed wise and could see that they were part of a parable.

Tig: Same as Tom-rig (*q.v.*), a class of butch fairies with the disposition of tigers. Some are good at fixing things like toasters, cars, or creaking barns. Others take things apart or remove critical pieces when no one is around so they'll never run again.

Tig Willow: A tree spirit and the fairest of fairies. Her wicker house is hidden in the crook of a willow on the edge of a silver river. She sees who passes by her green abode, but is rarely seen, except by girls on the cusp of their awakening. Willow is their first love, never to be forgotten.

Tipperty Fudge: An obscure fairy, either a clockwork Fairy-rat (*q.v.*), or a name for the Fudge Fairy (*q.v.*). Marion St. John Webb remarked:

> "Tipperty Fudge is my clockwork mouse
> Creepin' round an' round in the house."

Although Webb was under the impression that Tipperty Fudge was male, there is a tradition in Cornwall of Tipperty Candy, who loves sweets like mice love cheese. On Christmas, she steals all the candy in the childrens' Christmas stockings, but when she is stuffed and sick, she feels ashamed of herself. Before the children rise, she replaces the candy in their Christmas stockings with gold. She hates little boys, who like to set traps for her, as though she were indeed only a mouse. But she loves little girls, and sometimes moves into their dollhouses.

Tom-rig: A class of butch fairies. Some are large, some small. Knocky-boo (*q.v.*) is an auto mechanic tom-rig. Monny Wit Tig (*q.v.*) is a tom-rig that fortells the future. Tom-rigs often are associated with lions or tigers, or at least house cats. They are believed to be descendants of such ancient Lion-goddesses as Cybele and Sekhmet.

Tooth Fairy: A toothsome vampire. If you let her suck your blood at night, she'll leave a quarter under your pillow.

Tribades: Mortal girls whose family trees include a dash

U

Uggy Wuggums: The consort of Jammy Buggums (*q.v.*), elsewhere given as the consort of Bluecap Cowy (*q.v.*). She is the comeliest of all the Boggy-boos, called "Uggy" because the little toe of her left foot is twisty and weird looking. She is otherwise a perfect, androgynously beautiful fairy, frequently mistaken for an angel of god, by those who don't know any better.

Umbrama: Literally, "Mother of Shadows," an illusive nocturnal fairy who personifies secrets, and whose other name is Mysteria. At dusk she creeps from her silent lair and entwines herself with Zephyra (*q.v.*), the wind. They rut and coil about the mountain peaks, and slither through the valleys, manifesting themselves as titanic dragonesses. In the Land of Fair is preserved this mystic text:

"You looked into the shadows of my face sidelong, your black eyes hungry with a wicked light that licked across the skin of my cheek, burning. And I bared my teeth in a smile of slow perversity answering the hunger dancing in your eyes, on your tongue, across the quiet muscles of your naked shoulders. A long moment passed between us yet no muscle relaxed and I began to see the green and amber pitch of your serpent's scales flex out and ripple across your heavy breasts and ribs and uncoil down the length of your spine. Your entire body opened like a waterfall cascading diamond shaped scales from your crown to the narrow tip of your winding tail and I watched you roll towards me in a clashing symphony of iridescent green, cobalt blue and fire opal.

"As I turned to meet your thorny embrace, my raising shoulder blades exploded in a violent blaze and great silver wings shot up through flesh and fell in raven streaks against the wind. I leapt wildly at the midnight sky, moonlight catching in my feathered hair as the scars on my hands burst open to release coal black talons and I came crashing down in a full bodied fury against my writhing breast and locked your yellowed claws in a powerful grip. Feathers leapt like flames across my face searing down my back, below my belly, raging through arms and shoulders and burning into taloned fingers. I closed a burning palm around your throat and lifting your lips to mine I sunk my tongue along the cool whiteness of your sabered teeth.

"But you would not be held. Unfurling arms and wings in a river of moist heat beneath my belly, you scratched your jeweled tits against my feathered nipples, sunk your dragon's teeth into my open wing and pierced the very pulse of my heart with your black black eyes. Up you flew, twisting hips and tail round my thighs as you lashed from beneath me. Grasping currents on the air with your fish-tail wings you tumbled me beneath the savage folds of your rippling skin. I beat my silvered wings, fanned my tail and screamed from the very pit of my throat as your tail bound me against the cold ground and you sunk your fist into the black blood of my cunt again and again and again, your long blue tongue sinking and rising from the pearly fluids.

"And you drank and drank from the mouth of my sex until no blood was left to nourish, no voice to cast spinning into the stars above us and our bodies became parched of godliness. Scales and feathers vanished back into an older world and we lay woman's breast to woman's breast. Teeth, flesh and marrow of the bone remind us we are mortal after all and as you moved away I willingly conceded to your victory. But silently I swore that I would hunt for you across the city nights and when I found you

I would take what I had come for. And there would be no warning."

Umbrella: "Little Shadow Daughter." Women who honor Zephyra and Umbrama (whom see) walk beneath the shade of umbrellas, even on sunny days.

Ursalina: See under Xanthursa.

— V —

Vast: A giantess, within whose womb is the universe. She is also called Grandmother God, whom see.

Veela: Yugoslavian fairy-maidens who live in groups of three, or seven, or thirteen, related to the Elle-maids (*q.v.*) or the nymphs of Artemis. If they are spied by any man during their lustration ceremonies, rondals, and lesbian orgies, they will capture him and drown him, tear him into pieces with their strong hands, or shoot him with their arrows. But if a woman stumbles upon their midst, she will be taught to run on clouds and receive the gift of bow and arrows. Veela are so strong that one of them alone can knock over the walls of fortifications.

Vicky: In the Land of Fair, they tell of the descendant of Pallas Athena, the patriarchal apologist of ancient Greece. Vicky, though a mortal Christian, had fairy vision, and could see the gates of Fair. As a child, she set mousetraps at Fairyland's smallest doors. When grown, she built temples to the jealous, bearded Yahweh at the entrances to fairy caves. Then from pure ballsiness, she armed herself with an iron cross fashioned as a sword, and marched into the Fair Land, intent on slaying the queen. The fairies fell upon her at once, and instantly transformed her into a lantern filled with smoke. In this form, they returned her to her temple, where acolytes unknowningly swung her on a chain. Today, when fairies feel downtrodden, they cheer themselves in Cathedrals, watching Vicky swing.

Virginalia: Corruption of Vaginalia, the chief festival in the Land of Fair.

The Visit of Tiger Maid: This story was told to me when I was a young girl in Korea. Once the Tiger Maid came riding on a pony. She called at the house of a rich family and said, "An old woman lives on a hill in the forest. She has little food. Take her in, as that would please the ancestors."

"What would we do with an old woman?" asked the rich family. They threatened Tiger Maid with spears.

"Very well," said Tiger Maid. "I will flood the land from here to here." And she made a sweeping gesture with her arm.

That night was a terrible storm. Rain fell in such torrents, people thought a dam had burst in heaven. When morning came, the rain stopped, but the land was flooded, except a little hill. The rich family was ruined. They climbed onto the hill, spitting water. An old woman took them to her hut. "I haven't much," she said. "But have these." And she divided among them the last of her pickled cherries.

Here is another Tiger Maid story. Once Tiger Maid joined a secret society called the Blue Jades. They were women bandits. My own grandmother was a Blue Jade. I can remember them myself, strong beautiful women with swords and horses. One of them lived with grandma. She told me this story.

Tiger Maid rose quickly in the ranks of the Blue Jades. She fell in love with the leader, a mysterious woman from Manchuria who called herself Far Riding.

"You are my lieutenant," said Far Riding. "You must obey me, come what may."

"I will," said Tiger Maid. "But remember, I am the tiger."

"Very well," said Far Riding. "Take off your clothes so I can beat you with a rod."

"How have I displeased you?"

"Obey me, come what may."

"I will," said Tiger Maid. She took off her clothes. Far Riding beat her till her body bled, and Tiger Maid has stripes to this day.

"Now put your head between my legs."

"Like this?"

"Just so."

All night long, Tiger Maid took orders. But the next day, she left the Blue Jades and no one saw her for a long while.

A rival gang of bandits broke into the fort. The Blue Jades nearly lost the battle. Far Riding was wounded. She would have been killed, but that Tiger Maid suddenly arrived, and reversed the good luck of the rival bandits.

Afterward, she nursed Far Riding, who said, "I was cruel to you. Why return to save me?"

"I am Tiger Maid, after all," she said. "And for some while, I have loved you."

"I have loved you also," said Far Riding, "so I will tell you that I am actually Queen of the Northern Pillar of Heaven. Come with me to my country, and you shall rule at my side."

"I will," was the reply. "But remember, I am the tiger."

And that is why no one has seen Tiger Maid in Korea for a long time.

Vivien: Called also Nimue, the Lady of the Lake, consort of Morgan Le Faye (q.v.). In *Beowulf,* she is Grendel's Mother. She is related to Atargatis (q.v.) and Dictynna, the Cretan Huntress from whose name is derived the word "dyke." Vivien was the enemy of Merlin, stronger than he, and imprisoned him in ice (or turned him into thorns), although this legend has been badly corrupted through French variants. In her last incarnation she was the Poetry-fairy Renée Vivien, whose name means literally "Nimue Reborn."

Vulva: The Volcano-fairy, who is preserved in her more ancient Goddess form throughout Oceania (see Ocianna). In Europe and Russia she is the Chaos-fairy, named Anarchia, and attends terrorist action against tyrants. Women who honor Vulva construct small representations of her, using a rag, a bottle, and kerosene, and present Vulva as a gift for corrupt officials.

W

The Wandering Gentlewomen: A man wanted a male heir, but his wife produced three daughters. When they were still quite young, he took them in the woods and left them. They were unhappy for a while, but the Fair Women helped them, even though they rarely saw a fairy and had small notion of the source of their good luck.

They clad themselves in catskins. They lived wild and free but wanted to build themselves a castle in the forest, so they could be all the more happy together.

Their names were Meggy Caitskin, Tissy Caitskin, and Alexis Caitskin. They became expert huntresses, just as are cats, and did not mind living without a home. Still, they dreamt of a palace.

A flying Rat-fairy calling herself Fritzi Flüttermaus (*q.v.*) came to their camp one day and said, "Caits! Caits! Caits! Your sad, downtrodden mother waits! Woe! Woe! Woe! No lighty doth she know! Ow! Ow! The Awful Power! Has her locked in Yonder Tower!"

And so the outraged Meggy, Tissy and Alexis took up their ashwood staves with sharp points on them, and placed into their pockets numerous small asps, then took off through the forest toward Yawn Tower. There they heard weeping high up in its rafters. But there was no window, no door, no way in or out.

Within Yawn Tower the Mother of the Caitskins had been sealed for failure to produce male issue. Around the tower were placed six sentries. Fairies despise even numbers, so these guards were not apt to have good luck. Meggy

Caitskin shouted, "You and you! I'll crush your hat!" And though their hats were metal, and though they were brave if wicked men, she crushed their hats in just two blows, and both of them fell dead.

Alexis Caitskin shouted, "You and you! I'll smash you in the knees!" And though their knees had leather greaves, and they were tall and mighty fellows, Alexis hit each man twice, and all four legs were broken. They dragged themselves into the woods to hide, and there they died.

Tissy Caitskin called, "You and you! I'll make your codpieces jelly!" And though their codpieces were made of iron, and though these two men had proven themselves bold in many battles, they immediately threw down their swords and ran away to join a monastary.

Now the Caitskins tried to break the tower, but could not. An Ogre's magic held its mortar strong. And the Ogre was their father, who did despise all women, including those of his own family. This Ogre had heard the fighting at Yawn Tower and was even then riding over the mountain, bellowing with rage.

Inside the tower, Mother had grown quiet. The spell that held her imprisoned could only be broken from within, for indeed a stairway led to a simple handle that would open the hidden door. But she was under a *geas* or compulsion not to let herself out unless she received the secret signal, which only she and her Ogre husband knew.

"Mother, mother, can you hear?" called Meggy.

"Mother, mother, are you safe?" called Alexis.

"Pray, speak to us, mother dear!" called Tissy.

But within, their mother had grown silent. And the Ogre was fast approaching, shouting full of hate.

"I'll knock the tower over!" said Meggy, and smashed the wall with a fist, but the tower fell not.

"I'll knock the tower over!" said Alexis, and smashed it with her shoulder, but the tower fell not.

"I'll knock the tower over!" said Tissy, who kicked it with her boot, but the tower fell not.

The secret signal was three knocks, and having heard them, the Mother hurried down the steps and opened up the door.

They hugged in sweet reunion.

But the Ogre leaped from off his fire-breathing horse, and swore they all would die before he would allow his land and castle to fall into the hands of women. He took from his horse's saddle a long, barbed spear. But as he raised his weapon high, the three Caitskins drew the asps from out their pockets, and threw them at their father. The asps stuck to him all over, burning him with the acid of their poison. He went howling through the forest, screaming with agony, and for all anyone knows, he's running still, the asps stuck to his face and arms and groin.

Their Mother said, "Now we can all live happily in the castle."

"We cannot," said the Meggy Caitskin. "For many women need our help."

"Aye," said Alexis Caitskin, "but we will visit you on the Solstice and the Equinox."

"We will tell of our adventures," said Tissy Caitskin, "and you will be proud of us."

And that is the origin of the Wandering Gentlewomen.

Waps and **Thacks:** Two closely alligned varieties of Tigs (*q.v.*). They yell at one another and wrestle in public places, often in mud holes, usually for fun.

> The wiggedly Wap was wiffering wiggedly
> planning to whack the wimbly Thack
> The wimbly Thack is purple and black
> she calls herself Elinor — Elinor Thack
> Winny the Wap crawled out of a sack
> stalking the Thack that was taking a nap
> Thwack! goes the Wap; Yow! goes the Thack
> that leaps up to smack the wiggedly Wap
> Wiggedly Winny and Elinor Thack
> slapping so happily — *crickitty crack!*

When I Was a Priest: I awoke one morning and was no longer a handsome woman, but a priest. I put on my priest's garb and went into the chapel. There, a voluptuous woman was waiting to see me, and I thought to myself: "My gosh! To be a man at such a time as this, but only as a priest!" She threw herself at my feet and cried out, "Father! Why do we exist?"

"To die, my child," I told her; and she gasped, shuddered, drew away from me, then fell again in my direction, arms locked about my knees. "Father! Why have I had children!"

"So they may die," I told her gently, stroking her lovely hair.

Tears spread upon her rosy cheeks, cheeks shining in the votive candlelight.

"Why!" she demanded. "Why is there such suffering!"

"To prepare us for the worst," I told her soothingly.

"What can be worse than death!" she cried, clawing her way up my vestments, clinging with her strength.

"To die again," I said. "And again; and still again."

What a piteous note escaped her then! "If all of it is true," she pleaded, "then why are you a priest?"

And I replied, "To help you die."

Whether for better or worse, the next morning, I was myself again, and most unhappy, I knew not why. I sought a priest. He came to me in the chapel. "Father!" I cried. "Why do we exist?"

"To praise God," he lied.

"Why have I had children?"

"So they can praise God."

"Why is there such suffering!"

"So that in praising god, we can be happier than otherwise."

"Why are you a priest?"

"To help you praise God."

"God!" I cursed, and began to strangle him. "I hope you die!"

Wisewomen: Witches or wychts (*q.v*), hags and beggar-women, of all ages but the old ones are wisest, noted for their mystic knowledge, herb lore and gentility toward younger women. The Dim-dumpies (*q.v.*) were a wise-woman couple in England early in the 20th Century. Haggardly Beth (*q.v.*) of Scotland is said to have lived since the days of the Black Plague, and is still living.

Wisewomen have always been among us. In some eras they were honored, in others they were burned. In our own age they are forced to live despised at the periphery of society, selling blessings cheap.

The Wisewomen and the Wonder: Once upon a notion there lived a wisewoman in a wicker house on the bank of a crystal pond. Everyday she went out to talk to the fish and feed them bits of cheese. Everyday she kept a fire in the clay oven near her house, and made hardcakes from rye flour. Another wisewoman would visit to trade for cheese and butter. The second wisewoman was a dear friend whose name was Alistra, and the wisewoman of the wicker house was named Theora.

One day a fish told her strange news, and Theora was beside herself with fascination. She hallooed across the meadow and Alistra, who was younger and still spry, came to her friend's call.

"A boat is coming!" she exclaimed. "It will come up from the bottom of the pond!"

The two wisewomen sat on a fallen log and looked into the clear depths of the pond. Around them goats gathered, and nuzzled for attention. Theora patted them all, and called each by name. She pulled wet grass from the pool's edge and fed her goats by hand. An hour passed, and two; when the sun was overhead, the goats went to rest in the shade of the meadow's single tree. Theora and Alistra were alone.

So pure were the waters of the pond that they could see deep, deep into it; but there was no bottom. Fish of all sizes rose from the shadowy depths, then sank beyond view. Some of the fish were dumb and silent; some were wise as women. All of them were bold and terrible and beautiful. After a while, there were no fish anywhere to see, and Alistra said, "This is an omen."

"The boat is coming."

At first it looked like another fish, very small and very far down. It was even farther down than it seemed, for the fish was not small at all. In fact it was not even a fish. In a while the wisewomen saw that it was the prow of a boat rising from the lower reaches of the pond. Behind the prow stood a strange and wonderful being; and behind this being was a colorful, triangular sail.

The boat rose slowly, but wisewomen are always patient. They watched this wonder unfold and held one another's hands. After a while, the tip of the prow struck the surface; the boat came onto the surface with the water falling away from it and leaving it dry. It drifted in the middle of the pond. The being was not much unlike the wisewomen, except that its face was less serene and the chin was covered with fur. The being dressed like a wisewoman, in simple robes. For all the likenesses, the being was somehow very different from wisewomen.

A breeze filled the sail and brought this being near to the shore. The being said, "This is the beginning of a new age," and stepped onto the banks. The sound of the being's voice was deep and frightening. The grass where its foot stepped turned to ash. The goats leapt up from where they rested and scattered across the meadow, bleating in terror. An awful, fearful laughter bellowed from the being.

Side by side the wisewomen stood, and knew that it was no wonder but a catastrophe they were witnessing. They raised their arms, their four arms, and began to chant an ancient spell their mothers had taught them. It was a frightful, compelling spell that hurt them to say. But the wisewomen were strong, and they repeated the old chant over and over.

The strange being rose an arm as though to ward off a blow. It stepped back into the boat. The waters of the pond opened beneath the vessel. The boat sank, and sank, and sank.

"I must gather my goats," said Theora.

"I must tend to my rye," said Alistra.

Later that day, the fish who had told of the coming of the boat was found thrashing on the bank of the pond. Theora tried to save its life, but the fish pleaded, "Let me die," and Theora went away.

After many years had passed and the incident was long put from her mind, Theora was caring for her goats when a young girl came to her from the North. The girl said, "Mother, it is time to rest." And Theora taught the girl the ancient songs; and Theora died. When next Alistra came to trade flour for butter, she found a new wisewoman tending the goats, and they were close friends from the start. One day Alistra said: "Come with me! The birds have told me of a wonder! A kite will fall from the clear blue sky!"

And the young wisewoman followed the older across the meadow, to sit beneath the sky and await a wonder.

Wytches: Wisewomen, also called wychts. Wytches are, in particular, those wisewomen who have fairy blood and are therefore lesbians. Ben Jonson in "The Masque of Queens" wrote of a dame who joined eleven wytches:

> "Yes: I have brought to help your vows,
> Horned poppy, cypress boughs,
> The fig-tree wild, that grows on tombs,
> And juice that from the larch-tree comes,
> The basilisk's blood and the viper's skin:
> And now our orgies lewt's begin."

Wytches usually have about them something to do with the number thirteen. They may also have a third breast, sometimes on their thigh, for all fairy clans are loathe of even numbers. Wytches have many varied powers. Some believe a wytche can make herself small enough to use a thimble for a hat or an eggshell for a boat:

> "Don't break the egg, my dear,
> The wychts will make it a boat;
> Don't break the egg, for fear
> The wychts will sink in the moat."

A Bonny Wytche, or Couthie (*q.v.*), is said to be beautiful, whereas the Grim Wytche is a horrible hag. But some say these are not at all two strains of wytche, but only the double-aspect found within each individual wytche. The Gilly Wytche (meaning both guileful, and guileless) can be either good looking or ugly, depending on her mood or upon the perception of the viewer.

> "The gilly-wytche come rydin' in,
>   come rydin' in, come rydin' in
> The gilly-wytche come rydin' in
>   come rydin' in the mornin';
> I saw her! I saw her!
> I saw the gilly wytche.
> I saw her! I saw her!
>   Come rydin' on a switch."

Two Bonny Wychts who set up housekeeping together were remembered in a children's folk rhyme, preserved in *The Oxford Nursery Rhyme Book:*

> Bessy Bell and Mary Gray
>   They were two bonnie lasses;
> They built their house upon the lea,
>   And covered it with rushes.

X

Xandra: A spider fairy, related to the Norns and Fates, patroness of weavers and seamstresses. If her cobwebs are left unmolested, they become, over time, a fabulous tapestry, unbinding universal mysteries. Lesbians may enter her tapestry, as though it were a maze, exploring endless corridors and dimensions. Those who quest with love encounter Xandra on her golden thread, or before her spinning wheel, and receive a kiss of perpetual illusion. Those who come with anger find Xandra at her rack, and receive a kiss of death. Those who come in fear disintigrate her tapestry and are themselves reduced to scattered specks of dust and broken dreams.

Xanthursa: "The Golden Bear," a Mediterranean Boggy-boo, and sister of Yellow Martha (*q.v.*). Many legends are told of the Bear of Gold in mountain regions of Italy, Greece, and Turkey. One such tale has it that one storming night, a wet and frozen dark-haired maiden sought refuge in Xanthursa's cave. Xanthursa fed her porridge and warmed her in her bed. She and the maiden were thereby married, whereupon the maiden's hair began to turn to gold, and she became a lion. Xanthursa's consort is a remembrance of Aurora, who blinded Orion, for the Lion Maid is Queen of Dawn, and whosoever gazes on her shimmering tresses can never thereafter see ought but golden flame.

As Boggy-boos have generally a deformity of one kind or another, there are tales that say Xanthursa was bisexed, and that the Lion Maid gave birth to Xanthursa's daughter, Ursalina, the Baby Bear. A nursery tale describes Ursalina's tantrum. One day Ursalina threw her porridge on the floor, and broke her little chair. Granny Xanthursa would have punished her daughter, but that Ursalina ran into the sky. Even today, Xanthursa chases Ursalina round and round the heavens.

A very ancient myth provides us with the origins of this common nursery story. Ursalina, when a young woman, rebelled against the Lion Maid, striving to usurp the rule of Dawn. But her golden mother could not be dethroned, and she cast Ursalina into a blinding, fiery pit. To save Ursalina, Xanthursa sacrificed her ears, breasts, tail, teeth, and claws, tearing them from her body and placing them upon her lover's bed. But the Lion Maid would not save Ursalina, and Xanthursa died of grief. At the moment of the death of the bears, they were lifted up to heaven by the Lion Maid's remorse.

Xanthursa, the Lion Maid, and Ursalina apparently represent the three ages of women: maid, mother, and crone.

Xë: A lone, wayfaring fairy who skulks at the edges of fields, forests, and women's festive gatherings. Women occasionally catch sight of her out of the corners of their eyes, but she vanishes when gazed upon directly. Her mystery is great, and her purpose is uncertain, but there are some who believe she has wandered the world since very ancient times. She may be one and the same with the melancholy, tragic villain called the Nameless Stranger, who once nearly brought about the extinction of the fairies. During a celebration for the Queen of the Maiden Land, the Nameless Stranger brought into the sacred circle an antlered youth, who wounded the Queen so that she fell dying from her throne. The antlered youth then fled. Upon her final breath the fairy queen told Xë, "You must wait for me till my return." Xë, in a perpetual state of mourning, to this day waits at the edges of women's gatherings, perhaps defending women from the antlered youth.

Y

Yawwy: A nursery bogy of Fairyland. When little fairy girls are bad, mothers tell them, "I'm going to feed you to Yawwy!"

Yellow Martha: A xanthic fox-fairy, yellow instead of red. She transforms mortal lovers into red vixens and lives with them in the forests, where they run free, yelping and leaping with wild pleasure. If a consort fox-maid is frolicking alone and comes to peril due to human perfidy, she calls to Yellow Martha thus:

> "Help me, help me, help she said
> Before the hunter shoots me dead."

And Yellow Martha manifests herself as a great and golden bat that tears the hunter to pieces.

Yob: The obnoxious Yeast Fairy. She is uncommonly fond of moist dark places. Her enemy is Yog, the yogurt fairy.

Yuki Onna and the Woodcutter's Daughter: Far away in a certain place, upon a wintry mountain, a woodcutter's daughter was gathering sticks. She wandered farther and farther until firewood was stacked high upon her back. She worked so hard to find the fallen branches midst the snow, she did not realize the flurries had grown thick. It was impossible to find her way home in such a blinding storm. She dug a hole in a snowbank then set her stack of wood before it as defense against the wind. But gusts poured through the cracks, and the woodcutter's daughter shivered. She knew there was no hope, and prayed to the mountain spirits to look after her family.

Yuki Onna, the woman of snow, who stood in the heart of the storm, heard the piteous prayer of dying. She approached the pile of sticks, intent upon taking the girl's soul. The little stack of wood was scattered by her breath, and there huddled the frozen maid. Yuki Onna bowed to kiss the maiden's lips, and said, "Many times have I seen you wander on this mountain, with wood piled high upon your strong shoulders. Think not ill that I have taken thee in the flower of youth, for you will be with me upon the mountain's peak, and mortals will know you as the Blue Maid, who shares the power of Yuki Onna."

Yuki Onna and the Blue Maid lived happily for some while. But the Blue Maid became restless and dreamed often of the woodcutter's lodge and the little village nearby. In her dreams she heard her mother's lamentations, and it seemed as though her mother's presence grew fainter and fainter, until all that remained was an icy void. Yuki Onna, afraid her lover would waste away, gave the Blue Maid a lacquered box tied up with string, and said, "You may go to the land of the living. But when you miss our mountain abode and desire to return, only then, open this box."

The Blue Maid took the box, and it was like holding a block of frozen night. As she rushed away, Yuki Onna shed a crystal tear.

The Blue Maid sought the wootcutter's hut with ecstatic emotion. But all she found was a fallen ruin and weeds where once was garden. The leaves of the forest whispered, "Sasa-sasa." She called to her family members one by one but only the forest answered. With a horrible foreboding she hurried to the village, which she hardly recognized. She knocked violently on doors, but no one knew her. They thought that she was mad, and many feared her.

Only an ancient temple remained unchanged. In the cemetery nearby, she found the neglected grave of her mother. She fell upon her knees and wept. With mingled grief and anger, the Blue Maid lamented, "Oh audacious Yuki Onna, never to have warned me it would be so long!" In a moment of unthinking fury, she smashed the box of night upon a stone. A wind off the mountain sounded like Yuki Onna wailing with a pierced heart. And the Blue Maid vanished like a ghost.

A Buddhist nun strode amidst the graves at dusk. She came upon the ribbon and the broken box and knelt to claim them. Holding them to her bosom, she gazed about in astonishment, and whispered the name, "Yuki . . ."

Z

Zalmyra Halfleg: Zalmyra is the Giantess of Bald Mountain, thought to be of Cretan importation, and exceedingly ancient. One of her legs is a tree. She strides from peak to peak. She devours legions of men with her saw-tooth vagina, thereby enforcing peace. She breathes clouds and spits rain. A hundred thousand women live in the long coils of her hair and call her Forest.

Zany: Old Woman Laughter, almost certainly derived from Baubo, Greek goddess of jest, who tried to cheer up Demeter with lascivious verse and actions. Zany limps and hops about, reveals her pudenda, and tells peculiar stories. One of her tales goes thus: Two soldiers met in a field. They were enemies, but far from their troops. The first soldier said, "I would rather give you head than steel." They leapt behind the bushes, and are there yet. Another of her tales regards a heterosexual couple, for in the Land of Fair, nothing is so funny as a heterosexual. A man and woman were very poor, and each had but one treasure. The woman sold her enormous trousers to buy her husband ribbons for his beard, only to find that he had sold his beard to buy his wife suspenders.

Zedland Mox: A Serpent-fairy known in the West Country of England in 18th Century. She is unquestionably a late remembrance of the universal Serpent Mother worshipped since the Paleolithic era. She was reported throughout Devonshire, Somersetshire, and Dorsetshire. In this region they habitually replaced the letter "s" with "z," for which reason it was called Zedland. Fear of Zedland Mox ran so high, the people would not use a letter that looked like a snake, for fear the symbol would call her up.

Her true name was Siss, and the fairies called her Rabbit-chaser, because of her love of pregnant women. In the form of a ribbony snake she could slip under any door. Once within the house of an expectant mother, she would take on her aspect as a human midwife. When a pregnant woman moans while sleeping, 'tis said Mox has pleased her.

Zephyra: Wind-fairy, personifying women's souls. In her most powerful manifestations her names are Tempest and Hurricania. In Tibet she is a Giantess and yogini called Mother Mountain, whose breath brings storms and snow. Her consort is Umbrama (*q.v.*), Mother of Night, a fairy who was originally the holy ancestress of the Brahmins. As a universal fairy of the sky, she presides over Bird-fairies, Harpies, and wychts astride their brooms.

Zoe: In the *Apocolypse of the Land of Fair*, a book never seen by mortals, Zoe is the prophesized Last Born of Eld. Her coming heralds the end of the universe. To the Gnostics, she was the Creatrix who punished God for pretending to have made the world.